STARGAZING
BOOK 2
THE WALKER FAMILY SERIES

BY
BERNADETTE MARIE

This is a fictional work. The names, characters, incidents, places, and locations are solely the concepts and products of the author's imagination or are used to create a fictitious story and should not be construed as real.

5 PRINCE PUBLISHING AND BOOKS, LLC
PO Box 16507
Denver, CO 80216
www.5PrinceBooks.com

ISBN-10: 1631121294 ISBN 13: 978-1-63112-129-6
Bernadette Marie
Copyright Bernadette Marie, 2015
Published by 5 Prince Publishing

Front Cover designed by Bernadette Soehner
Photo by: Александр Савченко
Author Photo: Brenden Murphy 2015

First Edition/First Printing October 2015 Printed U.S.A.

5 PRINCE PUBLISHING AND BOOKS, LLC.

Stan,
Unimagined Brilliance.
That is what I see when I look at our lives.
It's as if I'm Stargazing.
I love you.

Acknowledgements:

To the five Stars of my life: I enjoy watching you shine. I love you to the stars and back.

To my brightest Star: You are my sun but you let me shine and for that I am forever grateful.

To my mom, dad, and sister: Thank you for allowing me to always let my mind wander into the stars as a child. I'll never outgrow that.

To Connie, Clare, and June: You are my trio of light. Just when it seems that the sun will set, it is you three that bring out the brilliance of my projects.

To my Street Team, my readers, and my fellow authors who bring me back to the computer every day to do what I love because they share their support with me…Thank you!

Dear Reader,

This book, like so many of my books, took me on a journey I didn't see coming.

Bethany Waterbury sure had a lot of skeletons in her closet. She was a challenge of the greatest kind as she fought back from a true, everyday demon which so many people fight.

Kent Black was the opposite. He was more fun, because he's an author. It's fun to look inside yourself and pull out those parts that are as important to the character as they are to the person who creates them.

I hope you enjoy this second installment of the Walker Family. They are so very different, each and every Walker. I look forward to what they will tell me each time I sit down at my computer.

Happy Reading!
Bernadette Marie

Other books by Bernadette Marie

STARGAZING

Chapter One

Hands in front of her chest, palms pressed together, Bethany inhaled as she pressed her foot to her inner thigh. Her body wobbled on one leg as she closed her eyes in an attempt to achieve her balance.

The Georgia sun glittered through the trees and the spring air filled her lungs on the patio outside of her bedroom.

She held the pose for five full breaths, letting the peace of the morning wash over her.

Letting her foot slide to the floor, she lifted her hands over her head, sucked in a deep cleansing breath and folded in half. Her spine gave a few pops as it lengthened.

The problem with this pose was she could see her toes were in desperate need of a pedicure. The next exhale was a sigh.

Bethany Waterbury stood, reached for her lemon infused water, and her towel. She wiped the sweat from her brow and sipped her water. In six hours, she had an audition for a commercial. This would be her first audition in nearly a year. Deep inside she didn't know what was worse, having done the horror movies she'd made in L.A. or wanting a grocery store commercial so bad she could taste it.

There was a tapping on her bedroom door.

"Come in," she shouted as the door opened and her roommate Susan walked in, a cup of coffee in her hand.

"It's beautiful out here today," she said as she joined her on the porch.

"It is. Still can't believe you gave me this room and didn't take it for yourself," Bethany admitted to her roommate who had given her the biggest room with the jetted tub and the patio.

Susan shrugged and sipped her coffee. "As soon as the house is built I'll have my own porch off my master suite," she said with a smile.

Bethany knew the day was coming. Susan would be moving in with her fiancé, who happened to be Bethany's cousin Eric.

Two months ago a psychopath, who had once had an affair with Bethany's mother, had shot Eric and burned his house to the ground before kidnapping Bethany. Weeks earlier he'd killed off Eric's animals and caused destruction to Eric's property and his grandfather's. It seemed as though Douglas had been obsessed with Eric's cousin Lydia as well.

She sipped her water again. Guilt still plagued her when she thought about it. Had she just stayed in California, where the magic of Hollywood had long given up on her, none of this would have happened to Eric.

It was her fault. She was the spitting image of her late mother. Just having seen her had set the man into some psychotic episode.

He'd been locked up and she'd been in counseling. When she'd come to Georgia, this wasn't what she thought she'd be doing. The point in moving was to bond with her father, not seek counseling because of it.

Okay, she'd bonded with him—a little bit.

He was a mess of a man, just as her mother had been a mess of a woman. Perhaps that was the common factor that had them together for the short time in which she was conceived.

Her father had a gambling problem, which had led him to using the family land as collateral to pay off his debt. His lack of discipline, of any kind, had nearly cost the family more than he already had.

There wasn't a lot of pride in saying she was Byron Walker's daughter.

"You look like you have a lot on your mind," Susan said as she walked out onto the patio. Her new diamond ring sparkled in the sunlight.

"I was just thinking about everything. My counselor says I can't blame myself for Eric's loss, but it's hard not to."

"He doesn't blame you. No one does."

"Just me."

Susan moved closer to her. "This is really bothering you."

"How can it not? I'm lucky that when Douglas shot Eric it didn't kill him. Or that he didn't die in the fire."

Susan knelt down in front of her and rested her hand on Bethany's knee. "Eric is fine. The house is framed. The stalls are full of horses and you are safe. Honey, you have to be able to move on."

She nodded. This wasn't anything that she hadn't been told already.

Susan stood and held out her hand to Bethany to stand. "What are your plans today?"

"I have an audition."

Susan's eyes grew wide. "Really? That's wonderful."

"We'll see."

"And you're going with me to Pearl's bridal shop this afternoon, right?"

Bethany had forgotten she'd promised to go wedding dress shopping with Susan. At least her sister owned the store. It was another step in getting to know her family—spending time bridal shopping would do that.

"I'll be there. Pearl is expecting us."

Susan sipped her coffee. "You're still able to work tomorrow, right? Lydia has us set to cater the book club dinner. They have Kent Black coming."

"Kent Black?"

"The writer." She held out her hand to gesture. "Haven't you read him? Oh, he's genius."

Bethany narrowed her gaze on her. "He writes science-fiction doesn't he?" she asked and Susan nodded. "Why would I read that? Why do you?"

Susan laughed. "I'm thinking you must be the only person who hasn't read it. It's been a New York Times bestseller for months. They're looking to make a movie of it. Hey, maybe you can put in a good word to him and he can suggest they cast you as Dessilla."

"Dessilla? Sounds like a role I was designed for." She blew a hair from her forehead. "I'm done with horror movies."

"No, she's a beautiful alien."

Bethany groaned. "I don't think I want to be an alien either. I'd better get ready. And yes, I'll be available for the book club."

"Good."

"How did she get him to come to the book club anyway?"

"I think she's more connected than we think," Susan winked. "I'll talk to you later. Good luck on your audition."

"Don't say that. It's bad luck."

"Right. Are you supposed to break a leg for TV too?"

"It'll do," she joked as Susan walked back out of the bedroom.

~*~

Coffee houses once were a source of inspiration. They had a vibe and a feel to them. Now, Kent thought, they were more like bars.

The same people walked in and out of the door every day. They ordered the same addictive concoction and either carried it out or sat for hours and chatted with others.

He missed the days where he could pull up to a table and no one bothered him for hours. Since he was traveling, it was one of his only options. Sure, he could hole up in his hotel room, but that wasn't very inspirational either.

Even though he'd rather be alone, he needed to surround himself with people for inspiration—he just wished they weren't so noisy.

The door opened again. It had become a habit to look up and study the person. This one had him sitting up, removing his fingers from the keyboard of his laptop, and following her with his eyes.

Long red curls bounced over her shoulders, which were bare in a sundress with yellow flowers. She was lean and toned and absolutely radiant.

She walked to the end of the line and Kent turned in his chair to follow her with his gaze.

She smiled at the boy behind the counter. Kent noted that the young man flushed at her simple gesture. That said something.

She continued on to pay for her drink. He heard the woman ringing up her order offer a pastry, to which the redhead waved off with her hand and a laugh. Obviously she'd avoid that, he knew just by looking at her. Her drink was probably low-fat blah too.

When she turned, the beauty of her hit Kent right in the chest. He'd never seen such a beautiful specimen.

She was scanning the room looking for an open seat. Wasn't it his very lucky day? The only free chair was at his table.

He stood, bravely—as bravely as any man who locked himself in his house and wrote about aliens could possibly be.

Quickly he wiped the crumbs from the front of his shirt and put on a grand smile, just as the redhead waved at a man across the room and headed toward him.

Kent slithered down into his chair and ducked behind his computer screen. He was used to that. Why should today be any different?

He took a Harry Potter movie pen from his Star Wars Celebration bag and jotted a note on the napkin on the table.

Redhead, glorious redhead in a yellow flowered sundress.

She'd live on forever, he decided, on the pages of his books as the princess he'd needed who lived in the far away galaxy of Vela Centauri.

Chapter Two

Bethany hugged her brother Jake and sat down at the table he'd claimed by the window. The coffee shop was unusually crowded today. Thank goodness he'd gotten there early.

"You look stunning today," he complimented.

"Thanks. I had an audition."

"Really? A movie? Here in Georgia?"

She laughed as she tucked her hair behind her ear. "No. Grocery store commercial."

He made an "O" with his mouth then sipped his coffee. "How did it go?"

Bethany shrugged. "Me, youthful and fit. The other twenty women, mid-forties with mommy bellies. Who would you trust as a spokesperson for a grocery store?"

"You didn't get it?"

"No. I should stick to horror movies," she tried to make light of it, but it nearly hurt to say it. "I'll just keep serving at Susan's catering events."

"Not a bad gig."

"No. It's been a good thing. I met a gal who owns a yoga studio too. I'm going to take a few classes and then she said when she sees my form, if it's good, maybe I can teach."

"Sounds like you're making your life here now."

"I think I am. I even have plans to have lunch with dad next week," she said, and swallowed hard.

His lips tightened. "Well, that's positive. He's hardly talked to me since Grandpa's funeral." Jake shrugged. "I take that back. He did need me to look at his car the other day. He needed a freaking oil change. That was all."

"Quite a contrast to Uncle Everett."

"I used to wish I was his son instead."

Hadn't Bethany even mentioned that she wished she'd been from the other side of the family?

"They have a unique bond," she said spinning the cardboard sleeve around the coffee cup.

"It's up to us to create that," Jake added. "He didn't do that for us. He kept you from us."

"Now I know why."

"But we didn't know. We had no idea. We just knew our moms hated your mom and they don't think highly of Dad either," he said referring to his mother and his sisters' mother.

"None of this is our fault."

"It's not. That's why we have to step up now and become a family. The five of us."

This was what she'd wanted—what she'd dreamed of her entire life. It was why she'd come to Georgia.

Bethany hit the button on her iPhone and checked the time. "I have to get over to Pearl's. Susan is wedding dress shopping."

Jake grinned. "I can't say I ever thought Eric would get married."

"They're good together," she said feeling the slightest pang of jealousy ripple through her. She'd love to find what Eric and Susan had found. But, considering she attracted psychopaths, the last thing she even needed to think about was men. Maybe she'd bring that up with the counselor tomorrow. Perhaps there was a standard time frame in which a victim was supposed to wait before they felt secure in dating—or even mingling with the opposite sex. Even the thought of it brought back the feeling of Douglas Brant's hand on her throat and the look of pure terror in his eyes when he shot Eric and set fire to the house.

"Are you okay?" Jake asked resting his hand on her arm. "You're as white as a ghost."

"I'm fine," she sucked in a breath. "I'm just fine. Sorry. I'd better be going before Pearl and Susan start looking for me."

He nodded, but she'd caused him alarm.

They both stood and she picked up her drink. "Thanks for the chat."

"I'm glad to have you here, Bethany. I really am. And I'm glad you're getting to know the girls," he offered, referring to their sisters. "I live in the same town and our mothers have always been friends, but to say we are family…"

"We will be," she assured him. "We will be."

Kent watched the redhead stand up and hug the man goodbye. There was nothing romantic in the hug.

He watched as she maneuvered through the tables and headed toward the door.

"Hey, Bethany," the man called after her and she turned. "Let me know how lunch with Dad goes."

Bethany! Could her beauty be any more enhanced than with such a gorgeous name?

"I'll do that," she said in a voice equally as heavenly. As she turned back toward the exit she caught Kent's eye.

He sat paralyzed behind his computer screen. Damn it, you idiot, smile—he tried to convince himself. Instead, Bethany smiled at him and kept walking.

He was blowing this!

The man was her brother. He'd nearly said that out loud when he mentioned their dad. There was no ring on her finger and she'd smiled at him.

As she walked out the door, Kent closed the computer and quickly tucked it into his bag. Trying to make his exit, he gathered all his trash and juggled it into his arms. Coffee splashed onto his shirt, but he didn't care. He dumped the trash into the can by the door and followed her to the parking lot, where she climbed into her car and drove away.

He let out a defeated breath. She was gone.

What did he really expect? Women didn't see him in coffee shops and drool all over him. Yes, he got lucky once in awhile and someone would recognize him, but they didn't vie to spend time with the geekiest man in a room.

He raked his hands through the mop of hair on his head. Before tomorrow's book club meeting, he should really get a haircut. After all, no one wanted to read the books by some slob.

He looked down at his shirt. First, he'd have to go to the motel and change his clothes. Hopefully he could find a shirt that was clean enough to wear. With more thought, maybe he'd better go to the Laundromat and wash his clothes. Living out of a suitcase didn't really offer him the luxury of looking his best.

Kent walked toward his beat up mini-van, which he'd bought from his sister for near to nothing. He tossed his bag into the passenger seat and looked around.

Macon, Georgia. It seemed like a nice enough place. The people had been pleasant. It was already getting warm, in early spring, and that made him nervous—what was summer like? But everywhere he visited could be a perspective home to him. He'd been homeless—so to speak—since he decided to live on the road and write his books. He'd thought it was going to be the adventure of a lifetime, but he could say, without hesitation, it had lost its charm.

However, as long as the money was coming in and they were still discussing the movie rights, he was going to live this dream. But again, Macon had a homey feel.

Maybe it was just the redhead—the glorious redhead.

~*~

Bethany parked across the street from her sister's bridal shop. She was there to support Susan, but there were a million other places she'd rather be than in a bridal store.

She'd never much cared for the institution of marriage. After all, her parents had never married each other. Her father had been married plenty and it hadn't seemed to work out.

In all honesty, she knew she wasn't even giving it a chance—marriage that was. There wasn't a doubt in her mind that Susan and Eric were absolutely perfect for each other and their marriage would last forever.

But never having had a married mother, Bethany wondered if she'd missed out on that want as a young girl. Her friends in elementary school would talk about playing dress up and they were brides. She'd attended more than one third grade, playground wedding. The bride, though, was never her.

Bethany looked both ways as she crossed the street. Before she opened the door to the quaint shop, she pushed back her shoulders and let out a long slow breath. This wasn't about her, it was about Susan. It was another moment to bond with her sister Pearl. An attitude adjustment was in order.

Once she felt as though she were in control of her feelings, she pushed open the door to the most girlie store she'd ever entered, *Pearl's Bridal Boutique.*

Bethany had no more opened the door and she saw her sister hurrying toward her. Her blonde curls were bouncing as she enveloped her in a hug.

Pearl held her at arm's length and looked her over. "You look beautiful today."

"I had an audition."

"I heard! How did it go?"

"I didn't get it."

Pearl's blue eyes turned sad. "I'm sorry."

Her long earrings shook with the shaking of her head and the bracelets on her arm clicked as she rubbed her hands over Bethany's arms.

"It's okay. Everything happens in its own time, right?"

Pearl smiled. "Right. And this time is carved out for Susan. I have a whole rack of dresses for her to try. Lydia is here too. I have a bottle of champagne and some delightful chocolate dipped strawberries. I'm just going to turn the sign around to closed and we can get started."

"You're closing the store for this?"

There was a glow to her sister, she decided when she looked at her.

"I'm so giddy to be with family I don't want anyone to ruin this. Besides, who ever thought Eric would get married and to a catch like Susan?" She grinned from ear to ear. "Audrey might stop by later," she said softly. "She's a little nervous to be around you, but I think she'll warm up just fine."

That thought twisted in Bethany's gut. She didn't want people to be uncomfortable around her—especially her family.

Pearl turned the sign and locked the door. Then she took Bethany's arm and led her to the back of the store where there was a bigger room full of mirrors, comfortable chairs, and more lace than Bethany had ever seen in her life.

Lydia stood the moment they walked into the room and moved in to hug Bethany.

"Oh, this is going to be so much fun," she said. Her dark eyes were wide with wonder as she pulled Bethany to sit next to her on the sofa in the room.

"I'll get the champagne. I have Susan trying on the first dress."

Pearl disappeared and Bethany took in the room.

"Have you ever seen so many dresses?"

"Only on the set of *Bachelorette Massacre*," Bethany commented with a snarl.

"You were in that movie?"

"It was my first. I was the second bridesmaid to get an ax to the head."

Lydia cringed and held her hand to her chest. "That's disgusting."

Bethany shrugged a shoulder. "It paid the rent. You can download it on Netflix I'm sure."

"No disrespect, but I'm going to pass."

Pearl walked back into the room with a silver tray in hand full of champagne flutes filled with bubbly, gold liquid. She set the tray on the table in front of Bethany and Lydia before handing them each a glass.

She held her glass in the air. "To the bride-to-be."

Bethany and Lydia raised their glasses and they all clinked just as Susan walked out of the dressing room.

"This is going to be the hardest decision I've ever made. I love this one and it's the first one I've tried on," she said with a quiver in her voice.

Bethany simply stared at her.

Her long dark hair flowed over her shoulders and the white lace of the dress hugged them. The bodice scooped in the front for a nice effect, but it wasn't too racy and the skirt opened fully.

Pearl set her flute down and walked to Susan. She picked up a padded bracelet of sewing pins and slipped it on her arm before tugging on the dress.

"It looks like this one would need a few inches off the bottom and just a little nip in the side here. You have a very athletic build."

"Not like Bethany's," Susan said as she examined herself in the mirror.

"You could do some yoga with me."

Susan's brows drew together as she examined the dress further. "I think I'll start tonight with your bedtime routine. Now would be an excellent time for me to be in the best shape."

Lydia sat with her legs crossed at the knee bouncing her foot as she sipped her champagne. "Your shape is nothing to scoff at. You could have tiny boobs like mine."

Everyone in the room turned toward Lydia, who now held her hands out to the side.

Yes, Bethany thought, Mother Nature has nearly skipped over that part for Lydia.

Bethany looked down at the V-neck of her own dress. She had plenty to share.

"Okay, go try on the next dress," Pearl instructed and sent Susan off to the dressing room to change.

"How many dresses do you have for her?" Bethany asked, noting the creeping sickness stirring in her stomach from what she assumed was nothing more than jealousy.

"Seven," Pearl beamed. "I actually didn't show her the last one. I think it'll be the one she picks."

Bethany drank down the champagne in her flute. This was her life now—the one she'd chosen to give into. Family was what she'd sought and this was what family did for each other. They suffered in a sea of white lace and frills just to make each other happy. She just wasn't sure she had it in her.

"Are you coming to the book club tomorrow?" Lydia asked.

"I told Susan I was available." Of course she was. She had no other life than to lock herself in her house afraid that some other psycho might decide to take his wrath of hatred out on her or her family.

"Kent Black will be there."

Bethany nodded. "I heard."

"Don't you love his books? He's a genius."

"You read that stuff?"

"Don't you?" Pearl added in surprise.

Bethany shook her head. "No. I don't. I read to enlighten myself. Learn something new. I certainly don't need someone's imaginary solar system filling my head. I have enough crap going on in there. Hell, I have a therapist."

Lydia pursed her lips. "That's not your fault. Don't ever think it is. Just because some maniac goes after you doesn't mean you can't open yourself up to possibilities. Christ, maybe you should read a book. You should read some raunchy erotic romance."

"Yeah, you know that one where…" Her words were cut short as Susan emerged again from the dressing room, and again, nodded at the dress.

"This one. This is it!"

Bethany smiled, but sat back against the couch. Seven dresses, and the one Pearl was keeping from her. This was going to be a very long night. Maybe she should pick up Kent Black's book. Perhaps it would put her right to sleep when she got home.

Chapter Three

Kent had driven up and down the streets near the coffee shop looking for the car that the redhead had driven. He'd seen one that he thought looked like it, but it was parked outside a barbershop and he was sure that wasn't where she'd gone.

It was useless. People floated in and out of his life. He was used to that. Some thought he was intellectually fascinating, while others criticized his thought process and said his creations were simply preposterous.

He wasn't some scientist. He never claimed to be. He was a guy who had a wild imagination and somehow it turned into a career.

That thought made him laugh as he pulled to the stoplight. What would his third grade teacher Mrs. C. think of his success now? She certainly hadn't appreciated his drawings on the back of his homework back then. *Kent has his head in the clouds again,* she'd say to his mother. *He's never going to be useful in society if all he thinks about are aliens and time travel.*

Kent looked in the seat next to him where a box of books sat. On the cover was a fantastic rendition of a drawing he'd done and Yance O'Connell had turned it into a mesmerizing piece of art. Yeah, Mrs. C. could eat erasers for all he cared. It might be funny to send her a check that could put her pension to shame.

The driver behind him honked his horn and Kent realized he was sitting at a green light. He eased through the intersection and headed toward the hotel.

He'd gather his laundry and then head out for that haircut he needed before tomorrow. Maybe he'd head back to where he thought he'd seen her car. It was the first actual barbershop he'd seen.

An hour later he was driving back down the street where he'd thought he'd seen her car, but this time he was looking for the barber pole.

There, on the right.

Kent slowed. There was an open space right behind the car he'd thought was hers. Whoever's car that was must work in the area.

He pulled into the space and parked. The basket of laundry in the back seat caught his eye now. He'd meant to find the Laundromat first so he didn't have to wait all night for his clothes to wash at the hotel laundry room.

Where was his head?

He knew where it was. It was with that redhead. Princess Carlotta, he'd named her in his book. Or he'd jotted down the name when it came to him. She'd be a very popular character. The teenage boys would want her and the girls would want to be her.

Yep, he was pathetic, he thought as he opened the door and climbed from the car.

A woman, as fine as the redhead, would come into his life someday. He'd been patient. He wasn't desperate. He was hopeful—yes that's what he was.

It was in his blood that was all. His parents had been married for nearly forty-five years and his sister was following right along in their footsteps. She'd been married now nearly seven years and had three kids. There was rumor they were thinking about another.

Kent had loved and lost. What girl wasn't impressed when he wanted to go to a Star Wars event for their "anniversary" weekend? Truth was, he hadn't found that woman yet. Zoe had shaken her head, rolled her eyes, and said she was done when he'd mentioned it. She had been his longest relationship. Two full years.

He laughed at himself as he stepped into the barbershop. There was no hope for him.

There was only one man cutting hair, but there were four old men sitting in the waiting area. None of them looked as though they needed a cut, he observed.

"I'll be with you in about ten minutes," the barber said as he cut the hair of the man in the chair. "Have a seat."

Kent wedged himself into the empty seat between a frail man resting his hand on a walking cane and a generously sized man who wore overalls of all things.

A TV in the corner of the shop was turned to a basketball game and all men were enthralled.

"Did you see that?" The man in the far chair slapped his hand on his knee. "Dad-gum!"

"Luck," another man said. "That boy has no skill."

"You bite your tongue."

"Oh, you think you know the game, Mr. Golf Pro?"

The large man to Kent's left laughed, but never took his eyes off the TV.

The debate continued until the man in the barber's chair stood, paid his bill, and walked out of the store. Kent figured he only had to wait out the next four men and he could leave—though this was a good opportunity for character development.

"Hey, kid. I'm ready for you," the barber said and all of the men looked at him.

"We're here for the game," the man with the cane said.

Kent nodded and took his place in the chair.

After telling the barber what he wanted he simply observed the men and their banter. It was fascinating.

The barber began the cut, talking to him and then talking to the other men. They were fascinated with the game and less than amused by Kent's career. It was refreshing, actually.

Midway through his cut Kent noticed the woman—the redhead in the flowery yellow dress. She walked across the street and to the car he'd thought he'd recognized.

"Whoa!" The barber said placing his hand on his shoulder. "You move like that again, I might cut your ear off, son."

"Sorry. I didn't...I saw..." He saw her car drive away.

The four men whose attention had been directed at the screen watched the redhead drive away.

"She's something," the man with the cane said with a whistle. "I'd have jumped from my seat too."

"California plates," another larger man said. "Must be lost this far south." They all laughed.

Kent hadn't even noticed the out of state plates on the car. Certainly she wouldn't be around town too much longer then.

"Friend of yours?" the barber asked as he continued on with the cut.

"No. Saw her earlier and she caught my attention."

"Can't blame you. You got Texas plates on your van. What has you here?"

Funny, they were equally as observant. "My job."

"Right. You write books."

Again, the man didn't sound impressed.

"Right," Kent repeated. The girl was lost, but tomorrow a group of book readers would be impressed by him. Lydia Morgan, the woman who had set up the signing, had been very fascinated by him—she'd said so. He could use some attention. Traveling alone—sleeping alone—eating alone was becoming, well, lonely. It was seriously time to think about finding a place or heading back to Texas. What were the odds there would be a *third chance is the charm* encounter?

When the haircut was finished, he generously tipped the barber, who whistled too.

"You come back any time," he said with a grin.

"If I'm in town I certainly will." He waved goodbye to the men and headed back to his pathetic mini-van.

Kent looked around for the promise of a Laundromat, but no luck. However, the store that the redhead had walked out of caught his eyes. *Crap!* A bridal store. He might as well go home to Texas.

~*~

At a stoplight, Bethany pulled her hair up into a ponytail and took a glance in the mirror on the back of her visor. She studied herself for a moment longer. Did she look happy?

When the light turned green, she closed the mirror and drove on.

She felt happy. She had new friends and was bonding with family. There wasn't a critical eye on her every moment judging if she was too tall, too thin, too redheaded. But something was missing.

Actually, she knew what it was. There had been this jealous buzz running through her since she'd arrived in Georgia after her grandfather's funeral. Her sisters were close to each other—and to their mother. Her brothers were close to each other—and to their mother. Even their mothers were good friends. Bethany stood out like a sore thumb.

Her cousin Eric had taken her under wing, but even he'd dubbed them the bastards of the family. His mother had past and so had hers. His father had married his mother out of pity, it had been said. Her father hadn't even married her mother.

She understood why now. Her mother's indiscretion with the psycho that tried to kill Bethany and Eric had her father keeping his distance from her for her own safety.

Officer Douglas Brant was locked up now. There was no reason to worry about him.

She was bonding with her sister Pearl and her brother Jake. Eric's fiancée, Susan, had become her best friend and his cousin Lydia had become a dear friend as well. It wasn't as if she were alone. Heck, she even had lunch plans with her father next week.

But still she felt as though something was missing.

Bethany pulled up in front of the house she shared with Susan and Eric. They'd planted some flowers in the pots that lined the walk and they were blooming. The buds on the trees were beginning to bloom as well. It smelled heavenly. Susan had already told her she could stay in the house as long as she liked once Susan and Eric moved back into his house after it was rebuilt.

The thought comforted her. She had a home. Even in L.A., where she'd grown up, they never really had a home. Her mother moved them from one friend's apartment to another depending on their financial situation.

Tears began to sting in her throat. She missed her mother horribly—though she really didn't know why. Perhaps it was because she had been all Bethany had ever had in her life.

Maybe that's what this gloomy mood was all about. Family surrounded her, but the one person that had always been there was missing. She'd passed away before Christmas.

She batted against the tears that threatened to fall. She couldn't go back now. This was where she was in her life. Tomorrow she'd don the apron that said *Susan Hayes Catering*, with the dangling strawberries on it, and she'd smile as she served at the book club. In time she'd etch out her own place in Georgia with her family. Everything took time.

The thought made her smile as she opened the door to her car and stepped out into the street.

A police cruiser turned the corner and slowed as it approached her. She knew Douglas Brant was locked away and it wasn't his cruiser pulling toward her. That didn't stop her heart from leaping into her throat and her hands from shaking.

The car pulled to a stop behind hers and Officer Smyth stepped out. He was smiling and it wasn't his sleazy, pick-up-on-you smile.

"Ms. Waterbury."

"Officer Smyth. What can I do for you?"

"I was just checking up on you. I saw you drive by."

"I'm fine."

"I heard Eric's house is almost finished. I'm glad they were able to rebuild."

"It'll be nice when it's done." She watched him take off his hat and run his hand over the rim. "Was there something else?"

He shrugged. "It's kinda childish really. I got word that you and Ms. Hayes were catering a lunch tomorrow for a book club."

"That's right. There's no danger to us, is there?" It was a silly sounding question, but the man who tried to kill her was a police officer. Her trust level was at an all-time low.

"No. No," he said shaking his head. "I'm a big fan of Kent Black's."

She let her shoulders drop. "You want a book signed?"

"It would mean the world to me."

"Why don't you just stop by?" She couldn't believe she was inviting him. Lydia was going to come unglued. The man had hit on her for years and she detested him. "I think he's going to speak for the first hour and then mingle and sign books the rest of the time."

He bit down on his bottom lip with his teeth and his brows drew in. "Lydia isn't going to like that."

"Don't ask her out then. I'll make it okay. Just come by."

His face softened. "I really appreciate this."

She actually believed he did. "No problem."

"You have yourself a good day. I'll see you tomorrow," he said, placing his hat back on his head and returning to his car.

Well, that was pleasant, she thought.

Bethany closed her car door and headed to the house. Kent Black, the name hummed in her brain. Who'd have thought that everyone she knew was into some sci-fi writer? She certainly didn't see that coming. What was the big deal about him?

She shut the door and set her bag on the table in the living room.

Susan's copy of his book caught her attention. The hardcover was protected with a shiny dust jacket. *Quantum a novel by Kent Black*.

She ran her hand over the raised front. There had to be six hundred pages in that book, she thought as she flipped the pages.

Reading wasn't her strongest skill, but as an actress she couldn't admit that. As a child, she'd struggled with dyslexia, but she'd fought that battle and won. Now she just had to take her time.

Bethany turned the book over and came face to face with Kent Black.

Dark hair. Dark eyes. Pale complexion. He stood with his arms crossed over his chest as if he was superior, but his face didn't convey that. He looked shy, that was it. As if the photo itself made him nervous. She couldn't help but think he looked vaguely familiar, but she certainly hadn't met him.

Bethany looked at her watch. Susan and Eric were going out to his parents' house for dinner and wedding planning. Bethany had turned down the invitation to join them. That meant she was alone all evening.

She weighed the heavy book in her hand. *Quantum* a nine-hundred-pound book by Kent Black, she humored.

Well, it was time to see what all the fuss was about.

Chapter Four

Bethany forced her eyes to open and they stung and burned. She rubbed them, even though her mother had taught her to never do so.

She looked at the clock on the table next to her bed. Ten o'clock.

The room was ablaze with sunlight and she jumped out of bed, nearly stumbling right into the wall.

She never slept that late. She'd missed doing her yoga, which had become her savior from bad habits she'd created living in Hollywood. She was supposed to help Susan finish packing up the catering job.

Hopping around the room, she looked for her slipper and then the other. Her hair flopped over her eyes and she scooped it back.

Damn that Kent Black. She'd picked up that stupid book at six o'clock last night and she hadn't fallen asleep until six in the morning. Never in her whole life had she read that much. The book was exactly five hundred and three pages long. But she'd been sucked in. She couldn't put it down. Her arms had grown tired and she'd propped the book up. She'd moved from the couch, to the chair, to the floor, to the tub, finally ending up in bed.

Bethany flung open her bedroom door and clomped down the stairs and into the kitchen where Susan turned with a gasp.

"What happened to you?" Susan asked, her apron already stained and a spatula in her hand.

"Kent Black!" She shoved her hair out of her face again.

Susan's eyes widened. "You have Kent Black here?"

"What? No!"

"Then what did he do to you?"

"I was up all freaking night reading that stupid book of yours."

"That's where it went," Susan said as she chuckled. "I thought I'd lost my mind. It was on the table."

"Was." Bethany nodded. "I've never read that much. I had dyslexia growing up and I'm a very slow reader, but last night I couldn't put it down. It sucked me in and…"

Susan was laughing. "I get it. I understand."

"I don't read sci-fi."

"Oh, no, I think you do now."

"I don't want to."

"Then don't do it again," she said, still laughing and turning toward her pan.

"I'll go get ready and help you. I'm so sorry I slept so long."

"Take your time. Glenda is coming over to help."

Bethany nodded as she retraced her steps up the stairs. Glenda, Eric's stepmother, had become their third person in the catering company. Really, she just wanted to bond with Susan and Susan was okay with that. Today it would be a blessing since Bethany obviously wasn't much help.

Maybe she'd give Kent Black a piece of her mind when she saw him later for keeping her up and throwing her off her game.

Bethany raced to her room, turned on her shower, and quickly ran a brush through her tangled mess of hair. She hadn't even put it up last night. It seriously might take an hour to get all the knots out.

She undressed and climbed into the shower, which was nearly scalding. Letting out a muffled scream she turned the water down, but too far, as she was nearly frozen. Did she really have time for this?

It had been a long time since she'd had such a morning, but usually it was brought on from something other than just reading.

Finally, the water was right and she began to wash the tangles from her hair. She scrubbed and shaved and washed her hair again, because she was quite sure she'd conditioned first and forgotten to rinse that out.

Today was just going to be a mess, she decided. Why did people purposely stay up all night and read books? She felt hung-over. This didn't feel much different than partaking in one of her mother's sleeping aids. A beautiful bottle of wine would have been a lot more fun.

Okay, that wasn't fair. She'd enjoyed the stupid book. She'd actually fallen in love with the main character, *Quinn Lamont*, she imagined him on a sigh. There was no need for her to be so worked up over having read it. It didn't mean she'd read his next one.

In fact, she thought if this was how she felt when she was done with the book, she would make a pact with herself. She'd never read another Kent Black book again.

Her hair felt silky. The tension in her shoulders faded away and she could breathe. That was better.

~*~

Kent didn't have that many clothes, but looking at them all strewn across the bed in his hotel room, he wondered what he was going to wear.

He'd tried to be edgy with a hip T-shirt. After all, when he'd gone to Comic-Con, the most influential people there were only in jeans and a T-shirt. Usually a printed T-shirt. He'd gone to a few panels where the speaker wore a Captain America shirt.

Yet, he couldn't make himself do it. It wasn't him.

He'd tied on four of his six ties and yet that hadn't appeased him either.

How was it he suddenly didn't know who the hell he was?

A glance in the mirror proved to him that he'd needed that haircut yesterday. At least one part of him didn't look as disheveled as he felt.

He pulled off the T-shirt he'd put on and slipped into a dress shirt. It was just nerves. He got them every time before he spoke in front of people and was forced to shake hands. Really, it was a crazy world for an introvert to put himself out there like he had. But that was the norm for writers. They were comfortable in their boxers writing stories that transformed the lives of normal people. They themselves were afraid of their own shadow, yet they put themselves on secret display.

It was part of the job, he reminded himself. He chose this path and it had filled his bank account nicely. Which had made his mother question why he'd bought his sister's ten-year-old minivan.

He was simple. He could admit that. There was no need for anything fancy. Usually those things just disappeared anyway. Someone stole them or they were ruined. A nice car would be no different. Seriously, who wanted a faded, gold minivan with a dent in the side door from a runaway shopping cart? No one.

After nearly an hour, he'd settled on a dress shirt and a sport coat—no tie.

For his own humor, he had a Superman T-shirt on under his dress shirt.

The book club was meeting in a place called The Garden Room. When Kirk pulled up in front of the building, it certainly wasn't what he'd expected. The outside looked like a refurbished warehouse. Sure, it was kept up, but it didn't fit the bill of what he thought a garden room would look like. He parked across the street. There was a sandwich board out front that said *Book Club, Featuring Kent Black*. He took a deep breath.

He vividly remembered the first time he read aloud something he'd written. Sophomore year in high school. He'd written a short story, which the teacher had been taken with. She'd asked him to read it in front of the class, much to his dismay. What if someone hated it?

Well, he got hit with someone's tuna sandwich from lunch before the class broke into hysterics.

It didn't stop the teacher. She had him in the teachers' lounge reading. That led to everyone in attendance writing him letters of recommendation for a scholarship—in which he received.

Who'd have thought they'd pay him to do this now?

As he stepped out of his van he caught a glimpse of a woman running toward a Subaru. Nicely dressed, short dark hair, and bright red lips. She opened the hatchback and pulled out an enormous tray covered in foil and then nearly dropped it trying to close the hatch.

"I'll get that," he called out as he looked both ways and sprinted across the street.

"Thank you, I…" The woman's eyes widened. "Oh, you're Kent Black."

Now it was time to put on the charm and act as if he enjoyed the attention. "I am, and you're going to spill your tray. Let me carry that for you. Are you here for the book signing?"

The woman placed her hands on her chest. "I'm Lydia Morgan."

"Then I guess you are. Nice to meet you."

"You have no idea what an honor it is to have you here."

"I appreciate that. Where are we taking this?"

"Just around the back. Susan, the caterer, is setting up. She'd forgotten this one tray. Her assistant is a bit late."

He gave her an easy chuckle, hoping to ease her a bit.

"I'll set this down for you and then go out and get the extra books in my car. I know you said you'd purchased some, but…" He stopped speaking when he turned the corner and saw an entire table full of books. "I guess you have enough."

"Most of them are pre-sold, but people have been calling all week. Don't bring yours yet, but we might need them."

Happy day, he thought as he followed her toward the small kitchen.

A woman with a long dark ponytail and a red apron arranged trays of dipped strawberries. When she caught sight of him, her eyes opened wide, just as Lydia's had.

"Hi." Her mouth turned up into an enormous smile. "I'm Susan. Thank you for your help," she said holding her hands up much like a surgeon would. "I'd shake your hand, but…"

"We can do that later. I'm Kent."

"I love your books. I'm sorry to look so stupid, but I'm very excited to meet you."

"Thank you. This all looks wonderful."

"Very simple garden affair," she said.

"I haven't seen a garden yet," he admitted and that had Lydia touching his arm.

"Come with me."

She led him through a room which he assumed would be used for banquets and receptions and out through another door which led to the outdoor *Garden Room*.

This time his breath was taken away. "This is magnificent," he said. "No one would ever think this was back here."

"Isn't it brilliant? My mother inherited some money years ago. Add that to her alimony my father paid, which we won't get into," she said on a laugh. "She bought this old warehouse and turned it into a hall. This is the first function in the *Garden Room*, which was my design."

"You did this?"

She nodded enthusiastically. "Bethany helped me choose what would go where. Her mother did some flower arranging and she's very good at it."

"Bethany?"

"Bethany Waterbury, perhaps you've heard of her."

It was his turn to be star struck, just by the name. "Of course I know who she is. I'm a huge fan of B-movie horror flicks. God, I've seen her killed in a dozen movies. She's brilliant. And beautiful—though I make that assumption since she usually has blood covering her face."

Lydia laughed again and her hand came easily to his arm, again. "She is beautiful and you'll love her."

"She's coming here?" The words croaked from his throat.

"Of course she is. She lives here now. She's Susan's fiancé's other cousin. I'm one too, but not related to her," she added with a laugh. "Why don't you make yourself comfortable. I'll get you a lemonade. I expect guests will arrive in about fifteen minutes."

He nodded as she retreated back into the building.

He pulled a chair out from the table beside him. *Bethany Waterbury.* She lived in Georgia and she was going to be at *his* book signing. What an honor.

Just for fun, he pulled his iPhone from his pocket and went to his IMDb app. He looked her up by name and more than a hundred pictures flashed on his screen.

The breath in his lungs caught and his hands began to shake.

Redhead, glorious redhead in yellow flowered sundress.
It had been Bethany Waterbury.

Chapter Five

People were already pulling into parking places on the street as Bethany pulled up in front of the building. She was already an hour late. She'd hardly helped with preparation at all. Her hands smelled of gasoline because she'd needed to fill her car or she wasn't going to have made it.

Finally, a parking space on the other side of the street appeared. Flipping a U-turn in the middle of the street, she pulled up to the space. Judging it with her car, she realized that the gold minivan had gone over the space by at least five inches. She couldn't get her car in there. Someone was not getting ice in their tea today, she decided as she pulled up to the next block to find a parking space.

She parked her car, opened the door, and climbed out as quickly as she could. Already her hair was coming loose from the ponytail and when she shut the door her apron was closed in it.

Breathe, she reminded herself as she opened the door, then cleared it before closing it and running toward the building where guests were already streaming in.

"Are you okay?" was the first thing Susan asked as she flew through the door. It was enough to have Bethany stop and take it in. "You're an hour late and I thought you were right behind me. Did something happen? You didn't get hurt did you?"

She should have known better than to not have called. After all that crap with Douglas Brant, everyone wanted her accounted for at all times. She couldn't blame them. The man had tried to kill Eric and she didn't want to think of what his plans for her had been. Besides, no one knew if he was the only one in town with some crazy obsession over her.

She willed herself to calm. Her mother would have taken a pill to calm the anxiety. Bethany wondered if they worked.

Bethany fixed her apron. "I'm fine. I stayed up too late reading and I seem to be discombobulated this morning. I stopped for gas too. I'm going to go fix my hair and wash my hands. I'm fine though and I'll be okay to work in about five minutes."

Susan moved toward her. "I'll always worry about you."

"I know. I didn't mean to make you."

Susan smiled at her. "You're here. That's what counts and you're going to love Kent Black. He's a really nice guy."

Bethany gave Susan a nod and headed to the bathroom. Yep, she couldn't wait to meet him either. This was entirely his fault. Her day would have been fine had she just done her yoga and went to bed. But no! She'd been sucked up into his book and now everything was a mess.

Kent smiled as a woman in a large hat shook his hand enthusiastically. "You have such a way with words," she said again. "I don't know how you come up with all those stories. You have sixteen books and they are all so different," she added as if he didn't know the statistics.

"Thank you. I try very hard to keep the reader engaged by coming up with new material."

The woman's husband was tugging on her to pull her away.

Lydia moved in before the woman in the red dress started toward him. "Can I get you anything?"

"I could use a glass of water. Maybe with a slice of lemon in it, if you don't mind. I knew better than to have lemonade before I speak. My throat is a little scratchy."

"Of course. I'm sorry. I should have thought of that before I brought it out."

He certainly didn't mean to offend. "Oh, it's okay. It was some of the best lemonade I've ever tasted. Homemade?"

Her smile softened. "That's how Susan works." She moved in closer. "Woman in red dress who is trying to get over to you is Mrs. Talbot. Widowed three times and thinks she's in her thirties."

He looked toward the woman who was clearly deep into her seventies.

"Does she really think that?"

Lydia shrugged. "Look at her shoes and her lipstick."

He glanced again. High heels at seventy. That was a risky move, he thought. His own mother was only inching into her sixties and didn't wear shoes that high anymore.

Lydia touched his arm as she left him and Mrs. Talbot moved in. Within seconds the woman was rambling on and moving closer and closer to him.

He hoped Lydia hurried back with that water.

"Mrs. Talbot moved in for the kill," Lydia said as she walked into the kitchen. "I need to take him some water. I gave him lemonade and now his throat is dry."

"Is he complaining?" Bethany barked.

"No. I think that's the problem. He wouldn't have. In fact, he loved it, Susan."

Susan smiled. "I'm glad."

Lydia filled the glass with ice and cold water from the pitcher kept in the refrigerator. She garnished it with a lemon wedge and handed it to Bethany.

"You deliver it. I think he wants to meet you."

"Me?" Bethany took the glass and stared at Lydia. "Why?"

"It seems as though our handsome author is a lover of the B-movie horror flicks."

Bethany growled. "They weren't all B-movies."

Lydia laughed. "I didn't mean it disrespectfully. He got excited when I told him you were coming."

"Why would you tell him?"

Lydia shrugged. "Your name came up when I was telling him about the room. I told him you helped me design it.

Bethany decided she was in sleep-deprived hell as she took the glass of water out to the Garden Room.

She didn't have to scan the growing crowd too hard to find him.

Mrs. Talbot was making her move on him. She'd moved in so close that Kent Black was nearly pushed up against a wall.

That's when she knew he'd seen her. His eyes widened and she could almost hear his plea for help. Perhaps she'd let him sit there a moment longer, but he took it upon himself to get out of the situation.

"Bethany?" he called as if they were old friends.

She felt the blood drain from her head. She didn't know him did she?

He moved quickly around Mrs. Talbot and straight to her. "Hi, sorry, had to get away from her. I'm Kent. I know you're Bethany. I'm a big fan. Not a stalker kind of person at all, just a big fan. I'm thankful for the water. That is for me, right?" She nodded and handed him the glass. "Thanks," he said as he took the glass and began drinking. "She's weird, that woman," he whispered. "Thanks for saving me."

"Do I know you?" she asked softly.

Kent took her arm and led her to the table at the front of the room. It was obviously a tactic to keep people from coming up to him, by keeping her close.

"No. Sorry." He set his water on the table and held his hand out to shake hers. "Formal intro now. Kent Black."

"Bethany Waterbury."

"I really like your work. I saw you the other day. I didn't know it was you, but I saw you."

She narrowed her eyes on him. "You saw me?"

"You were having coffee with some man. I think he was your brother."

"How do you know that?"

His cheeks flushed and he wiped his hand over his forehead. "Oh, well, the coffee shop was full. I saw you looking for a table. I was going to invite you to sit with me. You sat with some man and then when you left, you smiled at me, and then said something to him about having lunch with Dad."

God, he was a crazy mess too, this man who kept her up all night.

"You were watching me?"

"No. I was working. I observe everything and everyone when I'm working."

She thought about meeting Jake at the coffee shop. It was packed. They'd sat by the window. She'd left and…

"You were at the table by the door."

His eyes widened even more. "Yes."

"I do remember seeing you."

He was fighting some wicked smile, or his face was going through some transformation.

"You remembered me?"

"I do now," she tried to be stern in her delivery. "I think they're going to be ready for you to speak soon. It looks like everyone has filtered in."

"Right. Where are you sitting?"

She looked down at her apron. "I'm not."

"Oh, right. You're working with Susan."

"You're very good with names."

He sipped his water and she could see a bead of sweat form on his brow. "It's a gift. This speaking thing, it still takes some work."

"You don't like to speak in front of adoring fans?"

He chuckled at that. "Adoring? That's nice. I get nervous. Happens all the time. I'll start with my voice cracking and I'll make some joke about a frog in there. They all laugh. I have a mini heart attack and then I go on."

She couldn't help but ease at that. "I hate first takes. Perhaps that's some of the reason I don't have an acting job," she decided as she said it. "But I always freeze up on first takes."

There was a spark that lit in his eye when she said that. "You?"

"Why not me? You just said you did too. Barbra Streisand, I think it was her, said she had horrible stage fright too. Still does."

"I think I've heard that."

She'd eased around him and she certainly hadn't meant to. She'd wanted to give him words of anger for keeping her up all night. He was a little freaky with knowing too much too. So to ease up around him at all was not good, but she just couldn't help herself.

"You'll do great," she said making sure her smile reached her eyes. "It was a great book. I see why everyone is here."

She turned to leave when he reached for her arm.

"You read it? You read my book?"

"You've been meeting people all day that did that. Why are you so surprised?"

His hands tensed and he released her arm and flexed his fingers.

"Do you believe in fate at all?"

"No."

The expression on his face quickly turned to one of sadness. "Oh. That's too bad. I do."

"That's great," she said and turned to walk away again, only to have him reach for her, again.

"Can I show you something?"

"Mr. Black, now probably isn't the time."

He shook his head. "Nothing bad. Something I wrote that day in the coffee shop. I want to show you."

Bethany could almost hear Susan's voice in the back of her head calling for her, wondering where she was.

"Fine. But I need to get back to work."

She caught sight of Lydia coming toward them. This was her exit.

"I think we're about ready," Lydia smiled as she spoke. "Bethany, Susan is looking for you."

"I thought she might be." She gave Kent one last forced smile and hurried away to the kitchen.

Susan was loading up her tray to serve the first table their lunch. "I thought you ditched me. What's wrong with you today?"

"I told you. I was up all night. And then he caught me out there and wouldn't let me go. I know he was trying to get away from Mrs. Talbot, but…"

"You're rambling. Go get those plates out there."

"Right. Sorry." She picked up the tray and walked out to serve the first table just as Lydia turned the mic over to Kent.

Bethany set the first two plates on the table and looked up to the podium.

Their eyes locked and she could suddenly feel his pain.

A part of her had wanted him to stumble and make the joke about the frog. But then again, she wouldn't have wished that for herself.

Graciously, she gave him an encouraging smile, which must have hit him like a bolt of light to the chest. She actually saw him sway as he returned the gesture with a long blink, which she accepted as a thank you.

She continued on with her service as he started his presentation, without any mention of the frog.

Chapter Six

Kent Black had been talking and taking questions for over an hour and the book-loving crowd seemed to love him.

Susan and Bethany both leaned against the doorjamb watching him.

"He's eloquent," Susan said on a sigh.

"I suppose."

"Not as nice in person? You talked to him for a long time."

"He talked to me," she whispered. "He rambles."

"He'd never."

Bethany only shrugged as Lydia walked toward them.

"This is going so much better than I could have ever imagined."

"I suppose we should start cleaning up," Susan said.

"When he starts to sign, I think," Lydia added. "They're enthralled."

They all turned when another guest walked out into the garden and stood against the wall.

"What in the hell is he doing here?" Lydia asked as she noticed Officer Smyth.

"Don't get all heated," Bethany said standing up straight. "I told him to come."

"You talked to him? Why? Why would you do that?"

"He came by the house. I can't hate him entirely. He saved me."

"You saved yourself. He just had the power to arrest the ass who hurt you."

"Either way. He wanted a signed book and I told him to just stop by. Look," she said as she pointed. "He already has the book. He'll be in and out."

Lydia growled. "If he even so much as talks to me…"

"I told him not to ask you out."

Lydia winced. "I hate him."

"I know you do."

Lydia walked off as Kent finished his talk.

"You might owe her for that one," Susan said standing up and retrieving a tray as the crowd began to move about. "Maybe a girls' night out."

"Just for telling an officer of the law to drop by and get a book signed?"

Bethany watched as Kent sat at the table in the front of the garden, books piled high around him, and a line forming. Lydia moved to Smyth and escorted him to the front of the line.

Kent stood and shook his hand. Bethany had never seen Smyth smile a genuine smile. Maybe he did have some kind of heart in there.

Kent signed his book and Smyth turned to leave. He caught sight of her watching, gave her a wave of gratitude, and left.

Lydia moved back to her. "Fine. Done and done."

"Wasn't so bad was it? Look how happy he was."

"Don't care," she huffed and ran her hands down over her skirt. "Listen, I have to supervise. Do you think you could sit up there with him and help?"

"Me?" Bethany placed her hand on her chest. "I have a job to do."

"Right. He just needs books opened. Anyone who preordered or paid at the door has a slip."

Susan walked up behind her. "Go. You're too preoccupied today to be of much help."

Bethany let out a hurtful moan. "I'm here."

Susan's smile said more, though. "Go. Mingle a bit."

"Why? So someone can make a comment about me being Byron Walker's daughter and what a shame that is? Or they're sorry to hear about what happened to us and what a loser Douglas Brant is?"

"Or maybe you could just smile and help a nice guy out," Susan said with a gentle shove.

Kent worked the group as they came along. Each one had something to say about the book. Usually it was gracious praise, but there was always one in the crowd that wanted to know what he was thinking when he wrote a certain part.

Each question was met with a genuine smile. Everyone was a critic, but none as bad as he was on himself.

Bethany was walking toward the table now, no doubt working. However, she'd pulled out a chair.

"I've been sent to help you," she said as she sat down next to him and picked up a book from the pile.

He didn't have words. Just having her that close had rendered him nearly speechless. All he could do was nod and talk to the next person waving a book at him.

The next woman in line handed him a slip that said she'd purchased a book from the club. He turned to reach for one as Bethany turned to hand it to him. Their fingers grazed and there was a sudden spike in his blood pressure.

"Is that the right page?" Bethany asked, but he didn't even understand the question. "Is that the page you want them open to?"

He looked down at the title page of the book. "Oh, yes. Thank you."

She let go of the book and reached for another.

The woman began to talk to him and asked for a photo. He was on auto pilot now, which was good, since he'd suddenly gone numb in the brain.

This wasn't just being star struck with some Hollywood starlet either. He'd met his share of Hollywood elite. Four of his books had been made into movies. He had had a cameo in one of them, though once it had been cut to pieces, all anyone could see was the top of his head in a spaceship.

"Would you like me to take the picture?" Bethany asked as the woman contorted her body to take a selfie, which no doubt would give him a double chin and be posted on Facebook in the next ten minutes.

"Oh, that would be lovely," the woman said with a smile. "Would you mind if I took one with you too? You're Bethany Waterbury, aren't you? I'm a big fan of yours too. You're just as beautiful in person as you are in the movies. Oh, and your mother was beautiful too. I'm sorry to hear of her passing." The woman handed the camera to Bethany. "I was hoping you'd be here. I heard you were working for the caterer that is marrying the Walker boy. He's an odd one. Always so quiet."

Kent watched as Bethany smiled, just as he had at the woman. The strain showed in her eyes, but he figured he was the only one that saw it, since he was doing it too.

Bethany took the camera and snapped the picture of him and the woman. He then proceeded to take the camera and reciprocate the favor.

"Oh, thank you," the woman beamed and she clenched her book to her body. "You two make a lovely couple. It's kind of exciting to have a famous couple living here. I hope you'll be at more of these book club events. Lydia doesn't always invite the good authors. I don't always come. But if you two are there, I'll be here," she said on a giggle as she waved and walked away.

He heard Bethany let out a breath. "I'm going to get Lydia. She should be helping you. This isn't where I should be."

He reached for her hand as she stood to walk away. "You don't have to go."

"Oh, yes I do. Good luck with your signing and your book. It's very good."

In a moment she was gone and out of sight. He'd lost her again, but now he knew who she was and perhaps where to find her.

He smiled at the next person in line and signed the book, all while he thought of seeing Bethany again.

They had a spark of electricity—or static—between them. He couldn't leave Georgia without knowing what it really was. Homelessness now had its perk. He had nowhere to be but there—wherever Bethany Waterbury was.

Bethany nearly ran over Susan as she began to pack up totes and stack them by the door.

"Are you in a hurry?" Susan stopped her before she began to load the next tub.

"I just want to get out of here."

"What happened?"

She felt everything inside of her begin to unravel. "I don't belong here. People want to take my picture. I don't want to be that person anymore. I just want to hide here."

Susan's eyes widened and she gripped Bethany's shoulders. "Bethany, what's going on?"

Her skin was growing hotter. "I just want to go home. I'll help you finish packing up and then I want to go home."

"I've got this. Why don't you head back to the house? Eric should be there soon. Do you want me to send someone with you? Did something happen?"

"No. I just don't want to be around all these people."

Susan nodded. "Okay. Go home. You call me when you get there. I'll be awhile, but when I get home I'll make you some tea and we can talk."

She nodded in agreement, but she didn't want to talk. She just wanted to get away from people who called out her name and took pictures and...

Bethany held her breath and fought back her fear. No one was going to hurt her again. She was among family now. This was what she wanted.

"I'll meet you at home," she said as she picked up her purse and hurried out of the building.

An hour later Bethany sat in her car, parked outside of her sister's bridal shop. It wasn't her first choice for stops. She'd actually called her therapist first, but he was out of the office.

Maybe talking to a man wasn't what she needed either.

This was the first time in her life she was risking emotional failure on needing one of her siblings. Never in her life had she reached out to them for anything.

Pearl had been gracious to her. She'd made it a point over the past few months to include her as much as she could. This was new territory for her sisters and brothers too. They hadn't been included in each other's lives. She knew why now. That psychopath Douglas Brant had ruined Bethany's life long before she'd come to Georgia. Her father had been protecting her by shutting her out.

She stepped out of the car and walked across the street. Pearl looked up when Bethany pushed open the door to the store and a small bell chimed.

She smiled wide as she helped a young bride with a veil.

"I'll be a few minutes," she said.

"It's okay. Do you mind if I wait for you in back?"

Pearls eyes locked on her as if she knew something was bothering her. It was a sisterly thing, Bethany assumed.

"I have bottles of water and soda in the fridge. Help yourself."

Bethany made her way to the small room behind the counter. She opened the refrigerator and pulled a Coke out. Sitting down at the small table, she contemplated not opening the bottle for nearly a full minute. Her mother's voice rang in her ears. "No man wants a woman who lets herself go," she'd say to her whenever Bethany even thought of eating junk food or drinking soda.

Unable to go through with it, she replaced the soda and took out a bottle of water instead.

Pearl glided through the door as Bethany sat back down. Her sister was a sight, she thought. Her blonde hair was in a bun, or a twist—something fancier than what Bethany would do with her own hair. She had bands of pearls around her neck and her wrist and small diamonds in her ears.

Suddenly, Bethany was glad she'd reached for the water. The few strands of red curls that had worked their way out of the band that held her hair up, hung over her eyes. She quickly brushed them behind her ears. It was only then she realized she still had on the red apron from the event.

"So how was the book signing?" Pearl asked as she took a Coke from the refrigerator, opened it, and took a long, satisfying sip that ended with an "Ah!"

"Fine I guess. It's still going on."

Pearl pulled out a chair and sat down across from Bethany. "So what's he like?"

"Who?"

"The author. Kent Black?"

"Nice enough, I guess. He rambles when he talks. Observes too much when he's in a crowd. Has a dimple in his chin," she said with a smile and then pursed her lips to conceal it.

"Lydia promised to get me a signed book since I couldn't be there." Pearl took another sip of her drink. "So what brings you by? I didn't have you down for a fitting for the dress Susan picked out."

"No. I was just needing a sisterly moment I guess."

Pearl's eyes actually went moist, she noticed. "Oh," she said on a small gasp and smiled. "I like that. You look like something is bothering you."

Bethany opened her water and took a sip. Where did she begin?

"Kent Black is a really nice guy."

Pearl's brows lifted. "This is about him? Didn't you just meet him?"

"I did. And I'm not interested," she said convincingly. "It's just that…well…I realized that I'm scared."

Pearl reached for her hands and held them tightly in hers. "Honey, nothing is going to happen to you. Douglas is locked up."

"I'm not worried about him." she sucked in a breath and let it out slowly. "I don't want to be who I was anymore."

Her sister's grip tightened. "I'm not understanding. You don't want to be an actress?"

She shook her head. "No. I don't. I don't want to be known as Violet Waterbury's daughter. I don't want people to look at me and say *loved your movies*. It came with a price that I'm not happy I paid. I want to be…normal." Her voice shook and Pearl's eyes clouded with worry.

"What price did you pay?" her sister asked in a careful tone and Bethany's stomach began to clench.

"I shouldn't have come here. I don't need to drag you into this. I am who I am." She stood and turned, but Pearl reached for her.

"You're not leaving. Sit down. Drink your water. I'm going to lock the door."

"You can't close your business because your baby sister is in your back room crying."

"I most certainly can. Now sit."

Pearl disappeared out of the room and returned only a few moments later with a box of tissue and a plate of chocolates.

"I had a bride bring me these as a thank you. We're eating them."

Bethany stared at them as if they were the evil her mother had always spoke about. *You'll regret every bite you have.* She'd say before she herself would gorge on something, such as a plate of chocolate, and then purge later.

Pearl picked up one of the candies and popped it into her mouth. "Oh, Lord, that is wonderful. Here."

Bethany only stared at the plate. "I shouldn't."

"Um, yes, you should. We are having girl talk and this is what we do."

Her hand shook as she reached for a chocolate that was no bigger than the tip of her finger. Slipping it past her lips she let it melt on her tongue as if it were going to be the last thing she ever ate again.

Panic rose in her chest. The very thought of running to the bathroom to throw it up crossed her mind, but she forced down the vile feeling and the chocolate.

"Good, huh?" Pearl bit into another one and let out a moan. "Audrey would die if she knew I had these and hadn't called her to share them."

"Will she be mad?"

"No, she's just got a sweet tooth," she said on a laugh before she became very serious again. "Now, what's going on in that head of yours?"

Chapter Seven

Smiling all afternoon was exhausting, Kent thought as he sipped from the glass of water Lydia had brought him. The party was over. The guests had gone. But Kent was too tired to move.

Okay, who was he kidding. He was sort of hoping that Bethany was still there.

She'd left in a near panic when that woman wanted her picture. Shouldn't she be used to something like that? He wasn't offended. He'd wanted her autograph too, but he thought that would have been more awkward than their couple of conversations had been.

Lydia was walking toward him with a check in her hand. "Here's the money collected from the books you brought. I thought I'd ordered enough. I can't believe we sold your supply too."

"I'm honored that your friends thought that much of me."

"I had to turn people away from the luncheon. You're very talented, Mr. Black."

"I appreciate that. So does my mother. She's told me that for years when I've torn up entire manuscripts."

Her mouth fell open. "You've done that?"

"You see, I don't think I'm horribly talented. My mind wanders and a story forms. I write it down and by the luck of the universe, people seem to like it."

She blinked a few times. "I've never met anyone so talented."

"Thank you."

She handed him the check and he tucked it into his pocket without looking at it. That would have appeared untrusting.

"I guess I'll be on my way," he said fishing his keys from his pocket.

"Are you in town a few more days?"

He shrugged. "I go where the road takes me. But, I do like it here. I thought I'd stick around a few more days."

"I'd like to invite you out to dinner if you'd be interested. Susan and her fiancé, who is my cousin Eric, my brother, and another cousin," she said with a wave of her hand, "are going to dinner tomorrow. I know they'd love to meet you. If that's not awkward or anything. I'll bet you think I'm crazy now."

He laughed. "I think that sounds nice. The one thing about being an author is I can blend into a crowd. It doesn't seem that easy for Bethany."

Lydia clasped her hands. "What happened when she came to help you? She got upset and ran out."

He felt the hope drain from his body. So she wasn't there. "She left?"

"Yeah. She was very upset."

"Some woman recognized her. Asked her for a picture and told her she was as beautiful as her mother was. She didn't seem to like being recognized."

"I don't know her very well. Perhaps there is some reason she doesn't like that."

"You don't know her well? I thought you were related."

Lydia laughed easily. "I'm related to her cousin, but not to her. The Walkers and the Morgans have a very interesting dynamic. You know, the kind of things books are written about."

Now he laughed. "Maybe I should stick around and document it."

"Real life is always stranger than fiction."

"Very true." He picked up the book he had on the table. "Would you give this to Bethany? I was hoping she was still here."

Lydia took it. "I will."

"And I'd love to have dinner with you and your family tomorrow. What time and where?"

~*~

Bethany's eyes stung. It had been a long time since she'd cried that much in front of anyone. Was that what sisters were about? Pulling out your deepest, darkest secrets and holding you while you cried like a baby?

She'd had no intention of laying her life out in front of Pearl when she'd gone to her. She'd gone to bitch about her mother and about Hollywood's rejection—nothing more.

But now it was out there and Pearl knew all of her secrets. In Hollywood, they wouldn't have mattered. Everyone had the same secrets. In Macon, Georgia—that was another story.

She checked her face in the mirror. Hopefully, she could just run up the stairs and hide out in her room all night. Her cheeks were flushed. Her eyes were pink. The bun on the top of her head had completely given out and her hair was a mess of curls going a million different directions. This was her reality. This was why she'd come to Georgia.

She climbed from the car and headed toward the front door. When it swung open, she let out a yelp.

Eric stood there in the doorway, his arms crossed over his chest, and his brow furrowed.

"Where in the hell have you been?"

Bethany stopped on the step and simply stared at him.

"Where have you been?" he asked again in his demanding tone.

"I was with Pearl."

"Susan is sick with worry over you. She said you were coming straight home. You don't answer your texts or your calls. In light of recent events, you don't get to have the freedom to just wander where you want."

Bethany set her jaw and narrowed her eyes on her cousin. "You're not my father."

"No, I'm not. I give a damn a whole lot more."

"I'm twenty-four years old. I can take care of myself. And," she held up a finger, "I think that recent events prove that."

"It proves that when someone attacks, you can defend yourself."

"Well, it seems as though I'm in the wrong place at the wrong time then. I'll pack my stuff and be out of your way. I'd hate you to worry about me all the time."

"Don't you…" he started toward her when Susan pulled him back and walked out onto the porch.

Her eyes were damp and her hair equally as messed as Bethany's was.

"I was worried. I'm so sorry. I got him all worked up," she said as she pulled Bethany to her in an embrace that had Bethany gasping for air. "You were upset and out of sorts today. You didn't come home. I didn't know what to think."

"I'm fine," she finally replied and let her arms wrap around Susan, as Susan wasn't letting go any time soon it seemed.

When she did pull back she looked her over. "I'm going to worry about you. It's inevitable. You're my family now too."

"I appreciate that. I'm sorry I got upset."

"It's okay. You were at Pearl's?"

Bethany nodded. "I needed my sister." It felt good to say that and when she did it seemed like her burdens lifted a bit. "It was a long shot, but it worked out."

"Good. Good," Susan repeated as she stepped back and wiped her eyes. "I don't mean to treat you like a lost teenager. But, it would kill me if something happened to you."

"Nothing will happen. I can take care of myself," she promised and felt as that her tone conveyed it. She'd been doing it most of her life. Nothing in Georgia could ruin her if Hollywood hadn't.

Susan nodded and turned to go back into the house. Bethany followed, but was stopped when Eric moved himself in front of her.

"You didn't answer your phone."

"It died. I stayed up all night reading and I forgot to charge it."

"Douglas Brant might be in jail, but that doesn't mean there isn't some other lunatic out there."

"I understand," she said clearly and began to feel the chocolate in her stomach settle. "I'm okay."

"I'm your family too," Eric said as she tried to pass him. "I'm here. If you ever need me, I'm here."

She smiled. "You've been the best family I could ask for too. I promise to let you know where I am at all times."

He nodded as if that was a good enough answer.

It was a promise she would *try* to keep, but she wasn't used to people giving a damn about what was going on in her life.

She realized it wasn't fair to them, her attitude. After all, she'd come in search of family and she got it. Family worried. Family cared. Family loved.

Bethany made her way up the steps and to her room before the rejection of the chocolate finally presented itself.

She hurried to the bathroom and hunched over the toilet.

Family, she thought as she rested her head against the bathroom wall. Family would save her.

She jolted from her position when she heard the knocking on her bedroom door. This certainly wasn't where she wanted anyone to see her.

Quickly she flushed the toilet, so that it would make a noise and ran a towel over her face.

When she pulled open the door, Susan was standing there. She studied Bethany for a moment.

"Are you okay? You don't look well."

"I'm just super tired from staying up so late. I think I'll call it an early night."

Susan nodded. "Sounds good. Lydia invited us to join them for dinner tomorrow. Would you like to go?"

It didn't take but a moment to decide that she did want to go. She wanted to surround herself with family and friends. "I would."

"We'll talk about that tomorrow. Here," she said holding out Kent Black's book to her. "He gave this to Lydia. It's for you."

"Me? Why?"

Susan shrugged. "I don't know. He was looking for you to give it to you, I guess. Lydia said he seemed sad that you'd left."

Bethany took the book with a shake of her head. "He'll forget me by tomorrow," she said flipping through the pages. "He rambles."

"So you said." Susan smiled. "Get some rest. I'll see you in the morning."

Bethany shut her bedroom door and carried the book to her bed.

She turned the book over and looked at the man on the back cover. Now that she'd met him, she didn't think the picture did him justice. There was an easy feel to him, the picture was stiff. His hair didn't quite comb back the way it did in the photo, no, it looked as though he always had his hands in it. There was no sparkle in his eyes either and in person there was. The dimple in his chin was cute though and that thought had her setting down the book.

Seriously, she didn't need to think about the man at all. She'd met him. He gave her a book—that was very nice of him. But she didn't want to think about him in any other way than a static photo on the back of some book she'd decided to read. He'd be moving on from Georgia and heading out to his next thing. She'd still be there trying to piece her normal life together. They were going to make a movie of his book and she was going to consider giving up auditions for good. Maybe she'd seriously consider floral decoration. Susan had mentioned that she was good at it and it would come in handy for the catering business. Pearl might have a use for it too, with bridal bouquets and all.

Staying out of any spotlight seemed like the necessary course if she wanted that *normal* life.

Bethany opened the book and looked down at what Kent had written.

Bethany, it was a pleasure to meet you. I hope that our paths cross again someday. You're beautiful and intriguing. I'd like to get to know you better. Sincerely, Kent

P.S. Please call me if you're ever inclined to talk.

He included his phone number and a little smiley face. Softly she ran her hands over the words he'd written. Would it be so bad to be interested in someone, she wondered. She wasn't deserving of anyone special though. Behind her smile, wild mane of hair, and yoga poses there was just a messed up woman. No one wanted that.

But there had to be more, right? She looked at his name again. *Sincerely, Kent.*

Tossing the book to the end of the bed, she fell back onto her pillow. Stick to the path you chose, she reminded herself. Become who you want to be, not who you are, she repeated in her head as she closed her eyes.

Her body was exhausted, but her mind was wandering. She opened the drawer in the nightstand next to her bed and took out a bottle of pills with her mother's name on them.

She shook them. Thought about a full night sleep. Set them down. Cursed her life. Picked them back up, opened them, and took one. Just one good night sleep was all she was asking for. One night where she didn't think about the rejection Hollywood had bestowed on her—or the men who promised her the world just to feed their own needs—or the night Douglas Brant put his hands around her neck and she'd almost blacked out.

Bethany swallowed down the pill and it was sharp on her raw throat. She pulled the blanket up around her and closed her eyes. One—night—of—sleep, she repeated until she drifted away.

Chapter Eight

The phone didn't ring all night. Okay, except for Kent's sister calling so he could read a bedtime story to his niece. Then his mother called and told him about his grandmother's cat's new food. Lydia had called with the address and time for dinner. His father texted him and told him he liked the chapter he'd sent him—but Bethany hadn't called.

He looked at the list of recent activity on his phone and wondered if she'd gotten the book he'd sent her. She had said it was a good book, meaning she had read it. Maybe it had been a stupid thought to send her a book when obviously she already had one.

There were dark circles under his eyes because he hadn't slept well. He'd noticed them when he'd looked in the mirror that morning, before his first pot of coffee from room service. She was on his mind and he couldn't shake it.

He'd even gotten out of bed at one in the morning and searched Netflix for one of her movies just so he could see her. He watched her get killed in two movies before four in the morning.

This was a bad obsession. He had a tendency to do that. He'd meet some nice girl and get all wrapped up in her only to find that she only had been being nice to him, but was seriously not interested. Now what was he doing? He was chasing a woman who didn't even like to be recognized in public.

Okay, he wasn't chasing her. She'd simply been where he was. And the part about her having been at a bridal store should have set him a very loud signal. She was probably taken. That, and she didn't seem to have an interest in him at all. In fact, she looked at him the few times she had talked to him as if she wondered if he were going to stop talking.

God, he even rambled in his own head, he thought as he put down his phone and opened his computer.

He'd put out the DO NOT DISTURB sign so that the housekeeper wouldn't walk in on him in his boxers. He had another chapter to get written by the end of the day. If he planned on dinner with Lydia and her family, he needed to get it done.

He was just about to introduce a new character and her image was seared into his mind. The redheaded beauty, Princess Carlotta of the Vela Centauri galaxy.

~*~

It was nearly ten o'clock when Bethany stumbled from her bed. She was certainly hung over, but she'd accomplished exactly what she'd wanted to—she'd slept all night without dreaming of anything.

It had been a few weeks since she'd opened that bottle of pills. It was justified then, she thought as she placed her feet on the floor. Nightmares had consumed her. They'd started after the night Douglas had attacked her. Then it only led to parts of her life she'd rather forget playing out in her sleep. The first time she'd swallowed a pill not to dream was after she'd awakened to her mother's dead body—just as she'd found her before Christmas.

Bethany squeezed her eyes closed tight. She shouldn't have touched them. In fact, when her mother died, she should have thrown all the bottles away, but she hadn't. She wasn't her mother. There would be no taking too many pills. Bethany had her life under control. One night of rest here and there wasn't a problem. In fact, she'd throw them away, when she thought of it next.

For now, she was going to go for a run. She needed to work off that chocolate she and Pearl had eaten. She'd only had a few pieces, but that was enough to make her stomach pooch out just a bit, she decided as she stood and looked in the mirror. And if she was dining with family, she'd need quite a few miles and a nice long yoga session.

It was a good day for it. There were no catering events scheduled. She could have a carefree day.

Susan was seated at her computer when Bethany jogged down the stairs.

"Are you just getting back?" Susan asked as she turned to look at her.

"No. I got a really late start. I'm headed out. You want to join me?"

Susan laughed and lifted her coffee mug. "No way. My parents used to take ridiculous ten hour hikes. I think my rebellion as an adult is to not go outside and sweat. But you have a great time."

"I will."

"Oh, and dinner tonight is at seven."

"I'll be there."

"Why don't we just ride together? It's some new place Lydia invested in, I guess. Pearl wants to check it out to see how the wedding reception venue would be."

"Funny how this entire family can work anything into a business deal."

Susan chuckled as she sipped her coffee. "Speaking of which, I have a luncheon in two weeks. A bridal shower. Pearl set me up. Are you interested in doing centerpieces? You're super talented at it."

Bethany tightened the ponytail on the back of her head. "You're buying the supplies?"

"Of course. It would be part of the bid."

She gave her a nod. "I'd try my hand at it." She thought about it a little more. That might just be the calm she needed. No acting. No public show. Just her and a table full of flowers. "I'll be back in a few hours."

"Few hours? Isn't a run around the block enough?"

"Not for these thighs," she hollered back as she headed out the front door, shutting it behind her.

Bethany's run had been perfect and she followed it up with an hour of yoga. A long soak in the jetted tub in her room, and she was back to normal. There would be no need for sleeping pills tonight, she thought.

On her way home, she'd stopped by the organic grocery store and bought a salad. The thought of eating out was weighing heavy on her mind. She wondered what kind of food they would have. Certainly, they would have salads, but she was such a sucker for a big hunk of meat and dessert if it were presented.

Her willpower was horrible, which was why she was so worried about the meal at all. Would anyone notice if she didn't go? She'd been very social and really, she deserved to not be. People had hovered over her for the past two months. Would they really think anything about it if she didn't go to dinner one night?

Then again, she really did want to go. She loved Susan and Lydia. Any time she spent with Pearl was a delight. Of course Eric was more of a big brother than he was a cousin. She didn't want to miss dinner.

It would also give her a chance to be with Pearl in a social situation and prove to her that the breakdown she had at her store yesterday was a momentary lapse. She was fine. And because of that breakdown, she knew Pearl would have a scrutinizing eye on her. She'd eat her meal, just to prove that she could. Of course she could.

Bethany pulled the towel from her hair and raked her fingers through the wet curls. She'd be just fine.

With another thought, she opened the medicine cabinet behind the mirror and looked at the array of bottles she kept there. Maybe she'd take an appetite suppressant just in case.

~*~

"Does this look better?" Kent did a spin in front of his laptop which was balanced on the bed.

"You look fine. Have you never gone out to dinner with people before?" His sister laughed on the screen, her daughter cradled in her arms, asleep.

"I like it here and people have asked me to be social with them. I want to make a good impression."

"Who's the woman you're trying to impress?"

Kent loosened the tie around his neck. "No woman. Well, I mean I met one. She's totally not into me."

"How do you know that?"

"Bachelorette Massacre, remember that movie?"

His sister winced. "Yes. Horrible movie."

He shrugged. "The redhead who was the last one to die."

"The one in that horrible yellow dress?"

"Yeah, her. I met her."

"No way. Is she the one who's not into you?"

"Yep," he said picking up the computer and setting it on the desk. He pulled out the chair and sat down. "She works for one of the women I'm going to dinner with tonight, who is engaged to her cousin. And the cousin of the cousin is the one who invited me to dinner." He let out a groan. "Did any of that make sense?"

"Big family. I'm following."

"Yeah." He scratched his head wondering if he actually understood it all. "Anyway, she kinda gave me the cold shoulder. She might be getting married too. I'm not really clear on that. She was at a bridal shop."

"Maybe it was because of the cousin that's getting married."

He let out a breath. "Hadn't actually considered that."

"Yeah, I'm guessing she was already messing with your head. Which character is she going to be?" she laughed and then quieted when the baby stirred.

"You're not so smart you know."

"Which one?"

He let his shoulders drop. "The princess."

"I knew it." She looked at him from the screen. He was very thankful for Skype. "You look good. Maybe you'll find a place to land one of these days. At least you're making friends. Mom is worried you're just sitting in hotel rooms in your boxers."

He waved that off as if it weren't what he was actually doing. "I have to go."

"Okay, call me tomorrow. I want to know how it goes. Is she going to dinner too?"

"I didn't ask."

"Hmmm, yep, you're finally fitting in then. Look at you making friends."

"Goodbye, sis."

"Goodbye."

He closed the screen of his computer and smiled. Family was a good thing even when you weren't right there with them.

Chapter Nine

The restaurant was quaint. Bethany noticed that they did a high tea, which she hadn't done in years. It was something she and her mother would do for her mother's birthday. The thought filled her with a moment of sadness, but then she thought of the joy it would bring to start a tradition with her sisters and her new friends.

Lydia was showing Pearl the private room at the back of the restaurant. She sat down with Eric and Susan and ordered a glass of wine.

"I love that they have a lot of vegetarian choices," Susan said as she scanned the menu.

"I'm eyeballing that enormous steak," Eric added.

"You would," Susan said on a sigh as she reached for his hand. "I think your groom's cake should be a cow."

"Now that would be awesome," he said leaning in and kissing her gently.

A man's hand rested on Bethany's shoulder and she flinched as she turned to see Lydia's brother Tyson standing behind her.

"Sorry. Didn't mean to startle you." He gave her a wink and sat down in the seat next to her. "Where is my sister?"

"Showing Pearl around."

"My mom seems to have worn off on her. Now she wants to invest in everything."

"This is lovely," Susan said. "She has a good eye for properties."

"It'll be good for her. She needs to prove to my grandfather that she's as successful as she is strong willed. He still seems to be a bit of a chauvinist, even though I think she's already proved that she is a woman that can do anything she wants."

Pearl and Lydia hurried toward the table.

"This place is wonderful. And did you see that they do a high tea?" Pearl said enthusiastically as she pulled out the chair between Tyson and Susan. "Brides will eat that up for bridal showers."

"That's what I'm hoping," Lydia said taking the chair next to Eric. "In fact, I think we girls should do tea next week. Invite your sister Audrey," she said directly to Pearl. "And, Susan, you should invite Glenda," she mentioned Eric's step-mother.

"She would adore that," Susan sighed.

Bethany looked around the table and noted the empty chair next to her. "Are you expecting someone else?"

"I'm sorry I'm late," a voice came from behind her.

She turned to meet the equally as surprised glance of Kent Black looking at her.

"Hi," he said directly to her.

She wasn't sure if she'd even replied. It had never crossed her mind that he'd be joining them. And just as quickly, she remembered, that it didn't matter. He hadn't been the one to make her uncomfortable that afternoon.

She smiled and he pulled out the chair next to her and sat down.

"Kent, I'm so glad you could join us," Lydia lit up as she spoke. "You know Susan. This is my cousin and her fiancé Eric. My brother Tyson. Bethany's sister Pearl. And you know Bethany."

He was looking at her. "I do." He broke his gaze. "It's nice to meet you all. Thanks for having me join you for dinner. I've eaten everything on the menu at the diner next to my hotel. This will be a treat."

"How long are you in town?" Susan asked.

"As long as it takes. Or as long as I want. Right now I'm luckily homeless," he said as he crinkled up his face.

"Luckily?"

"Looking for that right place to call home. A perk of my job, I suppose. I can do it anywhere."

Pearl picked up the glass of wine in front of her and toasted him. "I like that idea."

The conversation continued about Kent's job and him in general. Quickly Bethany found herself easing back in her seat, enjoying family, a meal, and learning about the man to her side.

He was normal.

Kent was eagerly telling Susan about his sister's children. "Cole is five. He thinks he's Thor." That got a chuckle from the beauty next to him, but he didn't acknowledge her with a glance. He was keeping his cool. "Sara is two and also has an identity crisis. She thinks she's Elsa."

"Who is Elsa?" Tyson asked and looked around the table as if he were the only one not knowing. However, Kent thought Eric's look of confusion equally matched Tyson's.

"She's from Frozen." No recognition. "Disney Princess movie."

They both gave a nod, obviously accepting the fate that they had no clue or cared about.

"And her youngest is only fourteen months. Alyssa. So far she seems to know just who she is," he joked and Bethany laughed again.

This time he gave her a glance and a smile, which she returned.

It stopped his heart for a moment. She was exquisite. He couldn't help himself but want to get to know her better. This was the start to that opportunity. If he didn't somehow gum it up, that was.

"Do you see them often?" Susan asked.

"Every night."

"They live here?"

He smiled and shook his head. "Texas. We Skype every day. I read the kids bedtime stories. She helped me pick out my outfit before I left to come here."

Pearl sighed. "That is a very special relationship. You're very lucky."

"Don't I know it," he said softly and noticed that Pearl and Bethany exchanged what he'd consider an uneasy look, but the conversation Tyson and Eric started about oil wells quickly diverted any awkwardness.

Bethany had been around her family for nearly three months. She watched them all banter as she sipped her wine. They were easy to love and she had never regretted leaving California and staying in Georgia. Her only regret now was Pearl's glances toward her as she pushed the food around on her plate.

"Not a fan of green beans?" Kent leaned in close enough she could smell the hint of his cologne. "I'm not a fan of them either."

She let a chuckle escape. "I'm just a slow eater."

"My sister is too. Some nights we sat at the kitchen table for nearly two hours. The rule was no one left until everyone was finished."

"And yet you don't hate her?"

"Oh, I suppose I did for an hour and half, but otherwise, she's decent enough."

The smile that tightened her cheeks was genuine. "I missed that with my family. I'm glad you cherish it."

He was looking at her now as if there were no one else at the table. She looked at the others. Each of them were engaged in other conversations and she was, she supposed, engaged in one with him.

It wasn't so bad. If she'd loosen up just a little, perhaps she'd enjoy his company.

Bethany sat back in her chair, picked up her wine, and looked at him. "Who's older? You or your sister?"

"My sister is by fourteen months."

She'd lifted her glass to her lips, but lowered it. "That's not a lot."

"As kids it was great. She was only a year ahead of me in school. She's short, so my first growth spurt put me nearly four inches taller than her, which gave me the upper hand—or so I thought."

"Your mom must have been a saint."

"Still is. The most amazing woman I've ever known."

Bethany took that sip of wine now to ease herself. She wanted what this man had. All of it. She looked around the table and appreciated what the moment really meant.

She was getting a little bit of that normal that Kent Black knew all his life. It was just coming in pieces. So she wouldn't have childhood memories, but she'd have the ones from that moment on.

He continued to talk about his family and Bethany was captivated. She sipped her wine and he ordered another beer. When Susan got her attention to say they were leaving she realized that she and Kent had moved in so closely as they talked their foreheads nearly touched.

The expression on Pearl's face said she had noticed.

Bethany eased back and set her empty wine glass on the table.

They all pushed back from the table. Kent quickly maneuvered from his seat and stood behind hers, pulling it out.

"Thank you," she said as she brushed by him.

"My pleasure."

Outside of the restaurant everyone said their goodbyes. Lydia hugged and kissed them all, including Kent. Pearl shook his hand and pulled Bethany in for a hug.

"Are you okay?" she whispered in her ear.

"I'm just fine, thank you for asking."

"If you need me…"

"I know."

Tyson gave a wave as he walked to his truck and Kent still stood close by.

Eric held out his hand to shake Kent's. "It was nice to meet you."

"Likewise."

Susan moved in and hugged him as if they were old friends. "If you're in town for a while we should do this again."

"I'd like that."

They started toward Susan's car.

Bethany turned toward Kent to say her goodbye. Why did it seem so awkward as if there needed to be more? She should just shake his hand and walk away, but that didn't feel right.

"Thanks for joining us."

"No, thanks for letting me. I had a wonderful night."

"So did I," she said realizing it was airy and on a sigh. "I'll see you."

She finally turned to walk away, but he reached for her arm. "This might seem silly, but would you be interested in going out for some ice cream? I saw a little place not too far from here. I know we just ate a huge meal. I could drop you home after that. I mean, I know you don't know me, but…"

Bethany held up her finger. "Hold on, okay?"

His eyes were wide and he nodded. She hurried toward Susan who waited for her.

"I'm going to go with Kent."

Susan's mouth turned up into a wide smile. "You said he rambles."

"Horribly. But he just invited me out for ice cream."

That warranted a chuckle. "He's a nice guy."

"He is."

Eric walked back to them. "You're going to go with him?"

"Yes."

"We'll come too," he said tucking the keys in his pocket.

Susan rested a hand on his chest. "No, I don't think that's the plan," she said.

"We don't know him. I'm not letting anything happen to you."

"Nothing is going to happen. I'm okay," Bethany argued. "Ice cream and then he'll bring me home. I think I'm okay with this one."

She felt as though she were fifteen years old convincing her parents to let her go on a date. Or at least she assumed this was what that would feel like. There had never been any of those kinds of parameters in her life. At fifteen she'd already seen and done more on the Hollywood streets than most would in their entire life. Ice cream with a stranger actually sounded normal to her.

Eric's steely eyed glare made her uneasy, but Susan somehow managed to get him turned around and headed back to the car. "Call us if you need us."

Bethany agreed with a nod and walked back to Kent who waited patiently.

"Everything okay? He's very protective isn't he? We don't have to do this."

Bethany walked and Kent followed so they were headed in the opposite direction. "He's fine. He's worried about me and that's very nice."

"I'm not a weirdo or anything."

Bethany pushed her hair back over her shoulder. "You're not, but there are some out there. We had some drama a few months ago. He's just taken it upon himself to be my protector."

"He's a good guy."

"Yes he is," she said as they turned the corner and she realized she was hoping that Kent Black was a good guy too.

Chapter Ten

Kent kept his hands in his pockets as they walked the six blocks to the ice cream store he'd seen. He was having a bit of a surreal moment. He was walking down the street with Bethany Waterbury—on a date.

That might be a little too optimistic to think it was a date. Yesterday she'd run off on him—on everyone. There was nothing that would hold her back tonight either, he imagined.

When he got nervous he had a tendency to ramble, so he was concentrating very hard to not do just that.

Bethany had clasped her hands behind her back, pushed her shoulders back, and seemed to walk with a childish skip. Perhaps he had freed her a bit by taking her away for the moment. Whatever drama they must have had as a family, which she'd mentioned, kept them all a little on edge. Pearl's constant glances at Bethany hadn't gone unnoticed. Neither had Eric's protective stance.

The drama must have centered around her.

A lump formed in his throat. What could possibly have happened to her that kept everyone so on edge?

It was probably some fame thing. There were crazy people everywhere. Hadn't his own mother stumbled across the movie Misery and called him in a panic? She was afraid some fan of his books was going to kidnap him.

He'd tread lightly. There was no way in hell he was ever going to mention the horror movie marathon from the other night just so he could watch her. That certainly would put him in stalker status—especially with her family.

The shop was busier than he'd have liked at nearly nine o'clock at night. A warm spring evening must have put that in everyone's mind.

"We can go somewhere else if you'd like," he offered.

"This is fine. We'll just get it and walk around."

They stood in line and ordered. Unlike yesterday, no one noticed or recognized either one of them. That helped put him at ease.

Bethany ordered a scoop of mint chocolate chip in a cone. He winced. What a horrible flavor. He'd stick with good old vanilla.

They took their cones and headed back in the direction of the restaurant.

"This is really good," she said biting into the cold scoop. Watching her made his front teeth hurt.

"It is. Brings back memories of Friday nights at my house. My dad had a thing for ice cream. That was until the doctor told him to cut it out."

"I didn't have this with my mom," she said as she licked a drip from her finger. "She was always too worried about her figure."

"Your mom—Violet Waterbury?"

Her lips tightened. "Yes."

"I suppose the lifestyle in Hollywood is different. You don't hear of a lot of people being raised there."

She shrugged. "There's a lot of us. The focus isn't on family values though. At least mine wasn't. I certainly didn't have what my cousins did here."

"You weren't raised around them?"

She shook her head and took another bite from her scoop of ice cream. "No. My dad didn't marry my mom. My sisters are from one of his wives and my brothers from another. It's kind of messed up."

"It's not messed up. Just different from what I had. I sat with all of you tonight. I'd have thought you were a tight-knit family."

"I think we will be—in time."

"How long have you been here?"

"Few months. I came out after my grandfather died."

"I'm sorry."

She tossed her hair back again. "I didn't know him really. I'd met him a few times."

"So why come?"

"I needed a family," her voice dipped as she said it and he knew he was tumbling into territory he needed to tread lightly through. And since he was better at digging holes than treading around him, he decided he'd better come up with a detour for the conversation.

"I saw you the other day coming out of a bridal store," he said licking a drip of his ice cream that threatened to roll over his thumb.

"You did?" She stopped walking. "I thought you said you saw me at the coffee shop."

Kent pressed his lips together realizing he might have stepped right into that hole he'd dug. "I did." He wasn't going to tell her he drove after her to find her. "I happened to be at the barber shop across the street."

She nodded slowly. "Pearl owns a bridal shop. We were looking at dresses for Susan."

"That must have been it," he said trying to not seem as grateful as he was for the fact that she wasn't the bride. Of course, she wouldn't have been walking and eating ice cream with him if she were. "And did she find one? A dress?"

Bethany smiled and the apples of her cheeks lifted toward her soft eyes. "She did. It's beautiful. Eric is going to be toast when he sees her walking down the aisle." She licked the sides of her dwindling ice cream scoop.

"They've been together a long time, haven't they? They had a rhythm."

She looked at him and a crease formed between her brows. "A rhythm?"

"Yeah, you know when two people are just, well, perfect for each other. They anticipate the other's words or movements. They could talk without saying a word. Little gestures between them mean a whole lot more to them than to anyone who might have caught it. Rhythm."

The smile slowly faded. "I've never noticed that."

He shrugged. "I notice that kind of stuff all the time, but it's what I do."

"Right. And no, they haven't been together long. Eric has known Susan as long as I have. They met at my grandfather's funeral."

Now he knew his forehead was creased. "He picked her up at his grandfather's funeral?"

That eased the tension a bit. "She catered it. But I think his step-mother had plans the whole time. It worked out."

"What about you? Have you ever had rhythm with someone?"

The smile faded away completely. "No. Not with anyone. Not even my mother."

Kent stopped and turned toward her. "I'm sorry. I didn't mean to bring up anything bad. I keep doing that, don't I?"

"It's not your fault. Until a few months ago I didn't know that anything good truly existed." She began walking again and he kept her stride. "Susan moved here to start a new life after a divorce. She had it in her to be who she wanted to be and to get away from what wasn't working. She's my idol. I want to be that person. The one that makes a change when something isn't working."

"You moved here from California. Isn't that what you were doing?"

"Not on purpose. I was desperate. My mom died and left me with a lot of debts. I worked it off and thought maybe it was time I got to know my dad. Then I got here and, well, let's just say nothing works the way you plan it." She looked down at the last few bites of her ice cream and he thought she just might be sick.

"My car is in the next block. I'll take you home."

She stopped again, throwing the last of the cone in the trash and wiping her hand on the napkin before discarding it.

"I ruined your evening, didn't I?"

He stared at her. How could she think that? "Not at all."

"You were hoping for a night with the actress you enjoy watching. Not some nut job who doesn't even have rhythm with anyone."

He threw his unfinished cone into the trash and moved toward her. He wanted to scoop her up, but that didn't quite seem appropriate at the moment.

"I was hoping to get to know you, that's all." He stepped in a little closer. "Bethany, no one is perfect. You're young and you have a whole life ahead of you to find rhythm with someone and with yourself."

Willing himself even closer, he took a bold move and touched her hair. That wavy, red mane that absolutely was her calling card.

"You're leaving soon, aren't you?" she asked, her voice low.

"No time soon."

"Where I'm from, people come and go. No one stays forever."

"That's not how it works in my world at all." He brought both hands to her face and she didn't move away from him. This, he thought, was a very good sign.

"I didn't scare you away?"

He smiled. "You're afraid you scared me away? And here, after having seen your eyes glaze over when I talked yesterday, I was sure I'd scared you away."

"I didn't want to like you."

He leaned back. "You didn't want to?"

"Everyone was making a fuss about you. I didn't want to like you. I didn't have any intentions of reading your book either. But it sucked me in and then I was mad at you for keeping me up all night."

He laughed. He didn't mean to, but he did. "Were you upset that I wasn't the ass you were expecting?"

"Maybe," she said easing toward him, his hands still cupping her face. "You're very sweet and easy to talk to." She placed her hands on his chest and he was sure she could feel the hammering of his heart. He thought it just might explode.

"Sweet. I think that's a word I've heard too much in my life. It makes me sound like a sissy."

She shook her head. "No. I've never met a man like you in my life. You're not loud and boisterous. It's not all about you all the time. Your creative mind doesn't give you license to…"

He eased back. "I don't expect anything from you," he said. "Is that what men mean to you? People who are always expecting?"

"I've never known it any different."

"Bethany, I'm not like that." He thought it would be best to pull his hands back, but he just couldn't do it. "I don't care how many movies you've made or who your mother or father are. I want to get to know who you are. The real you. Not the one covered in blood."

She chuckled. "And you're not just some guy who lives his life stargazing and dreaming up new galaxies?"

"No. That's exactly who I am. I'm a great big nerd who seriously has thought about volunteering for that first Mars community."

She laughed—hard. "Oh."

"Are you the girl who is only covered in blood with an ear piercing scream?"

"No."

"Are you only Violet Waterbury's daughter?"

"No," the words were tighter.

"Who are you?"

Her eyes grew moist. "I don't know."

"I do. You're Bethany from Georgia. Young and beautiful and full of wonder. You're trusting. You're exciting. And right now you're in my arms and I'm not really sure how that happened."

Her body shook against his. "Are you going to kiss me?"

"I want to."

"Do it."

He kept his eyes locked on hers for another moment and then tipped his head to the side and moved in.

Chapter Eleven

Bethany gripped the front of Kent's shirt as he moved in to kiss her. His eyes had closed and his warm hands pressed against her face.

The world around her spun, much as it did when she took those pills with her mother's name on them.

She closed her eyes and let her body press against him.

His lips were pliant against hers. Warm and soft. Hungry yet gentle.

He didn't pull back with just a press of the lips. He deepened the kiss.

Kent's hands slid from her face, down her arms, and to her hips where he pulled her even closer. Lifting her arms around his neck, she opened her mouth to him and he took.

His tongue swept across hers and the moan that escaped between them could have belonged to either of them, but she was sure it was hers.

Kent's hands slid to the small of her back and pressed her even closer than she'd thought was possible.

Was this rhythm? She suddenly began to hope so, because with all the men she'd been intimate with, this topped the list. This one kiss was wildly passionate and gentle all at the same time.

She'd nearly forgotten they were standing on the sidewalk as people drove by.

Kent eased back, but his eyes didn't open. He looked as though he were holding on to the moment, just as she was.

"I seriously didn't expect that," he said, opening his eyes and gazing into hers.

"It was nice."

"It was more than that." He stepped back, taking her hands in his. Lifting them to his lips, he pressed a kiss to each one. "Tell me I can see you again. I'm not used to women kissing me like that. I might just be lightheaded enough to think you might."

Her insides were in a knot and she found herself having to press her hand to her stomach. "I'd like to see you again."

Kent's mouth turned up into a warm smile. "Good. C'mon, I should get you home before your cousin starts searching the streets looking for you."

Hand in hand they walked down the street to the restaurant they had dined at. Stopping in front of an old minivan, he pulled his keys from his pocket.

"This is your car?"

He winced. "Yes."

"Not what I'd expected."

"What did you expect?"

How did she tell him she expected anything other than a minivan? "I don't know. I thought only people with kids drove minivans."

"Or people who just need a reliable car. I bought it from my sister. I can honestly say if I'd thought I was going to drive a beautiful woman around I would have at least rented something nicer."

She liked him. A day ago she didn't want to, but she did.

"I think it's just fine," she said as he opened the door.

"The bonus is I've had it detailed every three months. No milk stains or French fries in the seat. That makes it a bachelor's car."

"Well, then, I guess it is the perfect ride." She slid in and he closed the door.

The interior smelled of him, his musky cologne and shampoo. She sighed as she took inventory of the tingles that raced through every inch of her body. She wasn't going to let him go home. She was going to wrap him up in her arms all night long and make him promise to never leave. Once she was done with him he wouldn't want to. No, he'd be the first one to want to stay forever, especially since he didn't want anything from her.

Kent opened the door and slid into the car. "Okay, directions please."

She gave him the address. "Easiest way is to go down about six blocks and take a left."

"Where does everyone else live? Around here?" he asked as he pulled away from the curb.

"I live with Susan, but as soon as their house is finished, she'll move out to Eric's."

"Where does he live?"

"His family lives about forty-five minutes out of town. Twenty minutes on dirt," she said with a chuckle. "Lydia and Tyson live out that way too."

"And Susan and Eric are building?"

Bethany gripped her hands tightly in her lap. "His house burned down a few months ago. So they are rebuilding."

Kent shifted a glance at her and then back to the road. "It burnt down? Was anyone home?"

She swallowed hard. "He and I were there. No big thing. We're both okay." She wasn't going to tell him the story of another day when she just wasn't perfect. There had been enough of that for one night.

"I'm glad you're okay," he said as he reached for her hand and laced his fingers with hers.

She sat and looked at their hands rested between them. When was the last time someone had held her hand like this? She couldn't even come up with a time. Had no one ever just reached for her?

She could fall in love with this man. It was possible, she thought. He'd run. He'd run fast and he'd run far. The fact that he didn't even live in Georgia should have sent her a million signals to let go of his hand and say goodnight when he dropped her off at the door.

They didn't say much more on the drive, but he never dropped her hand.

When he pulled up in front of her house he told her to wait. He hurried around the car and opened her door. She might have swooned when she stepped out and took his hand.

"This is a cute place."

"Susan has an eye for it. The inside is very bright. Would you like to come in?" she asked, and hoped, as he walked her to the front step.

"Yes, but I'm not going to." He pulled her in tightly and pressed his body to hers. "I'm going to kiss you goodnight and head back to my place cursing myself for not going inside. But I wasn't raised like that. I'd like to ask you to dinner tomorrow though."

A part of her ached from his rejection, but the other half of her realized it was a blessing. For the first time in her a life a man wanted to do more than just *her*. Kent Black was a gentleman. She'd never met one and she was sure she was going to mess this up expecting the worst from him.

"I'd like that."

"Good," he let out a breath. "I'll pick you up at seven?"

"I'll be here."

He took his phone from his pocket. "I'd better get your number and give you mine. Just in case you change your mind."

Who was he kidding? It would be him that changed his mind in time.

She took his phone and typed in her number. "Text me when you get to your place and I'll have your number."

"Good idea," he said, slipping the phone back into his pocket.

He stood on Susan's front porch just looking at her, but she didn't fear him. Men who stared at her wanted her or something from her. Sure, she was confident that there was a spark between her and Kent Black, but he didn't just want her body or one night. If he did he'd have taken her invitation. There was more behind those eyes.

"Can I kiss you goodnight?"

"I'd be disappointed if you didn't," she admitted, as she stepped in closer to him, wrapping her arms around his neck and letting him pull her in until there was no air between them.

Again, their mouths pressed together and she took possession of him this time. The moan was distinctly his. His hands remained in the small of her back, flat-palmed, holding on for dear life. She tangled her fingers into his hair and sent their tongues on a dance that again had her head spinning.

They were breathless when they parted. She nearly asked him inside again when he stepped back from her.

"I have to go. I'll see you tomorrow," he said with a wave and a quick step away from her. "Seven."

She nodded and watched him open the door to the car.

"You have to go inside. I'm not allowed to leave my date at the door without seeing her inside," he yelled from the street.

God, how did she get this one?

She gave him another wave and let herself into the house. The sound of his car driving away was only heard after she'd closed the door and fallen against it.

Kent Black. What had he done to her? He'd made her want again—for more than just affection.

"Was that Kent that just left?" Susan's voice came from the dark living room.

Bethany pushed away from the door and walked toward the room.

Susan turned on the small lamp on the table beside her.

"Yes," Bethany said on a very obvious sigh, which she hadn't meant to let out.

"You had a nice time?"

"Yes."

"You're swooning."

What the hell? She might as well sit down and tell her all about it.

"He's taking me to dinner tomorrow," she said as she curled up on the couch next to Susan.

"That's wonderful. You hit it off."

"We did."

"Are you still mad at him?"

She shook her head. That had really been a dumb fit to throw. "How could I be? He's a real gentleman."

"A real family man too," Susan added.

"He drives a minivan. That was not a turn on."

"But you're still interested?"

Bethany rested her head back against the couch. "I am. I don't want to be, but I am."

"Why wouldn't you want to be?"

"My life is complicated right now. This is no time to get worked up over a man."

"I don't know about that. Maybe it's the perfect time. Not all men are Douglas Brant. They don't all want to hurt you."

She believed that, but Douglas Brant hadn't been the first. It was going to take awhile to trust that even Kent Black wasn't only out for sex or power.

Though, his refusal to come in tonight should have made that clear.

"I don't think Kent is the kind of man to hurt anyone on purpose. But some day he's going to leave Georgia. He doesn't live here."

"Enjoy it until then and who says you can't go with him?" She patted Bethany's leg. "Okay, I'm going to bed. Eric wanted me to wait up for you."

"He doesn't have to worry about me."

"He always will. You're his family." She blew her a kiss and walked up the stairs.

Bethany sat alone and let the silence envelop her. She wondered if Kent would wait up for his sister too. There was no reason to think otherwise.

He was a good man.

It was time she got to know what that was like. She closed her eyes and just enjoyed the natural buzz still tingling in her body. She was relaxed, calm, and very tired.

Chapter Twelve

I made it home safe and sound. No one kidnapped me or even tried. It's quite disappointing, his text to her read.

Kent tapped his fingers on the top of the small table in his hotel room waiting for her to answer.

Do I know you? JK! I'm glad you're safe. It would have ruined my dinner plans for tomorrow, was her reply.

He ran his fingers over the screen as if it would pull her in closer to him.

I like your sense of humor. I can't wait for tomorrow night.

Her text was quick. *Neither can I. Goodnight, Mr. Black. Sweet dreams.* She added an emoji of a happy face blowing a kiss and he could feel his entire body warm with just the thought of the goodnight kisses they'd shared.

Goodnight.

No more texts went through, but Kent held onto his phone as if it still connected them.

His sister would throw a fit if he called her at midnight in Texas, but he was dying to tell her all about Bethany. Instead, Kent pulled out his laptop and composed a detailed email. She'd call when she got it.

Sitting back in his chair, he replayed the night in his head. After the signing, he'd been sure he'd never see Bethany again. What a very nice surprise to find her seated at that table and next to the empty chair.

Letting out a long and satisfied breath, he tucked his hands behind his head and kicked his feet up on the coffee table. That kiss on the street was the most intimate kiss he'd ever had with a woman. Which made him nervous too. Had he been that bad of a lover, if this was the best kiss?

No. It just meant this kiss meant more. But why?

The red hair and green eyes were stunning, that was no surprise. It didn't make her though. There was something deeper that made Bethany Waterbury who she was.

He'd already figured out that she wasn't very trusting, didn't believe in fate, and way out of his class. But deep inside of him, he didn't care. He wanted to get to know her—the Bethany no one else knew.

There was backstory and he wanted to know it. Why was she not raised with her father and her cousins? Why wasn't she going back to California to pursue her career? Why did her body mold so perfectly to his when he held her in his arms?

All he had was time, he thought, as he sat up and placed his feet on the floor. There were a few more stops on his book tour, one of them was in Texas only thirty minutes from his family. But then he thought he'd return to Georgia. He simply wasn't done getting to know Bethany Waterbury.

~*~

Moonlight streamed through the window and patterns, from the blowing tree limbs outside, created moving murals on the wall.

Bethany watched the designs change as she wished for sleep.

Her heart was still fluttering, her body buzzed, and the kiss between her and Kent played over and over in her head.

Men were always interested in her. It was part of her *former* career. But no one had ever made her feel quite like Kent had. She wasn't sure what to do with her feelings.

As sad as it was to admit it to herself, she was more comfortable with men wanting her just for sex and power. She understood that.

Pure, unadulterated interest—she wasn't sure what to feel.

It was nearly two o'clock in the morning and Bethany just couldn't lay there any longer. She needed her sleep.

A cup of tea would be helpful. Perhaps a few yoga poses.

Bethany bit down on her lip when another thought crossed her mind and she sat up. Brewing a cup of tea would take ten or fifteen minutes.

Yoga was always a great way to relax, but she simply wasn't motivated at the moment to unroll her mat and go through the motions.

Swinging her feet over the side of the bed, she wrung her hands together. So what if she couldn't sleep. She could download one of Kent's other books and read. It would be as if he were with her. But she was beginning to shake just feeling the need for sleep.

Quietly she walked to her bathroom and opened the cabinet behind the mirror.

A sea of golden hue bottles with white tops lined the shelves. Each bottle was labeled VIOLET WATERBURY and she had promised herself she'd throw them away. But tonight she needed their magic. She needed to sleep.

Bethany looked at the labels and found the one she knew would give her a few hours of uninterrupted sleep. Maybe half a pill wouldn't be bad, she thought. It would just take that edge off and give her some rest.

She opened the bottle and poured out one pill.

One pill would give her hours of rest, but no. She would only take half.

Sticking her fingernail into the groove on the pill, she managed to split it in half.

She slipped it between her teeth and swallowed it down then chased it with a handful of water from the sink faucet.

Without hesitation, she put the bottle back into the cabinet and closed the door. Looking into the mirror she tried to see past the dark circles under her eyes and the hollowness in her cheeks. It was late and she was tired. Again, she promised herself that she would throw the bottles away in the morning. But for now she was going to get some sleep.

The only problem with sleep brought on by a pill was how hung over Bethany felt the next morning. She rubbed her eyes and stretched, only to feel twice as tired.

There had been no dreams—and she'd hoped she'd dream of Kent.

Rolling out of bed she pulled off her pajamas and slipped on her running shorts. She'd better get in a few miles before it got too hot.

As she jogged down the stairs she could hear pans rattling and dishes clanging in the kitchen. Susan was up early.

She poked her head around the corner. "You're busy already."

Susan spun to look at her. Her hair was a mess piled atop her head and her apron was covered in flour.

"Nice that you could finally get out of bed. We have a catering job at one. Did you forget?"

"No. I'll be back in time to help."

Susan's eyes widened. "It's eleven. I've been busting my ass all morning because I couldn't wake you up. You were sleeping so soundly, you didn't even hear me when I stood over you and talked to you. I even touched you trying to wake you. I need you to be at this luncheon."

Bethany stepped into the kitchen and looked at the clock. "I'm sorry. I thought it was only six."

"Are you kidding me?"

"I'm sorry," she stammered as she backed out of the kitchen. "I'll go get ready."

She hurried up the stairs and stumbled through her room, and to the bathroom cursing herself the whole time. It had been a bad idea to take that pill. God, what if she'd taken the whole thing?

Susan had never let her down. She couldn't betray that by letting her mother's medicine cabinet dictate her life.

Bethany turned on the shower, stripped down, and opened the cabinet. The bottles, all in their line, sat peacefully as if to offer her comfort. But they weren't. They were demons, just as they were for her mother.

As tears began to roll from her eyes and down her cheeks, she pulled the bottles out and threw them in the trash. She didn't need them. They offered her nothing in return but heartache and pain.

They had taken her mother from her. Why had she kept them? Why had she ever even used them?

When the trash can was full, she stepped into the shower and let the pain of it all wash away.

No more, she promised herself. She was going to free herself from her vices. No longer was she a Hollywood starlet, or even a want-to-be. She had a family who loved her in Georgia and that was where she was staying.

As she tipped her head back into the stream of hot water she thought of Kent. She had him too, she thought. Certainly that meant she loved him. She'd never been in love before, but when someone consumed your thoughts, that was what it meant, right?

Now she felt the anticipation of need for him rise in her chest. Seven o'clock couldn't come fast enough. She needed Kent more than she ever needed anyone.

Chapter Thirteen

If it could go wrong, it had. Bethany had heard the unmistakable sound of Susan's door slamming when they got home. She hadn't even unloaded the car, as she diligently always did.

Bethany's hands shook as she carried in the first tub of dishes. Her head spun and beads of sweat trickled down her neck. It was six o'clock. She'd get showered and ready for dinner. She could wait till then to eat as she hadn't all day.

For now, she'd finish carrying in the catering tubs and try to make up for the disastrous afternoon, which she had been mostly to blame for.

Bethany made two more trips from the car to the kitchen before she heard the front door fly open.

Heavy footsteps hurried into the house and a moment later Eric was standing in the kitchen.

"Where is she?"

"She ran upstairs to her room and slammed the door."

He stepped in. "What happened?"

"Eric, I'm sorry."

His eyes narrowed as he inched further into the kitchen. "You're sorry? What did *you* do?"

"I made us late. I didn't help because I overslept and then she forgot items that had been my responsibility." Bethany ran her hands over her pant leg. "I dropped a serving tray full of food," she said as the tears began and wouldn't stop.

"Hey," he pulled her into him and held her. "Now things go wrong once in a while. It's okay."

He pulled back and looked her over.

"Are you feeling okay? You look a little pale and skinny."

That caused her to snort a laugh. "I'm fine. Pale and skinny are normal where I come from."

"They're not normal here," he said taking her hands and looking at them. "You're shaking."

"I haven't eaten today."

"You eat. I'm going to go check on her."

"I'm going with Kent to dinner. I'll eat soon."

Eric nodded and started for the stairs.

She called after him and he turned back. "Tell her I'm sorry. I never meant to hurt her. I understand why she had to let me go."

He walked back toward her. "She said that?"

Bethany bit down hard on her bottom lip as she nodded. "She has no choice. I understand that."

He touched her cheek. "I'll talk to her."

She watched him walk away and knew that she deserved to be fired. How could she blame Susan?

A glance at the clock told her if she didn't get her ass in gear she was going to be making Kent wait for her too. It was a trait she wasn't too keen to have. Her mother was always late. She lost countless jobs over it too. No, Bethany wasn't going down that road.

~*~

"I like the blue shirt. No tie," Kent's nephew said.

"Ties are nice."

"Nope."

He laughed as he removed the tie and looked back at his computer. "Better?"

His nephew shrugged and ran off in another direction.

His sister laughed. "I liked the tie."

"I'll think about it." He picked up the computer from the dresser top and walked toward the window, setting it on the small table. "Do you believe in love at first sight?"

"I believe in being alone so long you think it's love at first sight," she said.

Kent sat down and thought about that for a moment. "I don't want that to be the case."

"You don't get to decide that."

"Sure I do," he said putting the tie back on. "She makes me feel like I've never felt before."

"And that's why you're dating. You go out in public a few times and see what you think about each other and then you spend some time alone. Kent, there's no need to rush anything. You just met this woman."

He nodded as he finished the knot. "She doesn't like people to recognize her."

"Then don't take her anywhere where they will. Keep it low key."

"I want to bring her home."

"Mom will think that's pretty serious."

Kent clucked his tongue. "I know. Maybe it will be."

His sister picked up a wandering toddler that happened by. "Tell Uncle Kent to have fun on his date."

Instead he was blown a kiss and that was even better, he thought.

"I'll let you know how it goes."

"If it ends early enough, they'd love a bedtime story. But if it goes well, don't call too late."

"Wouldn't dream of it. Bye, sis."

"Bye," she said as he closed his laptop and stood to examine himself in the mirror.

He wouldn't consider himself a catch by any means, but Bethany seemed interested. How that happened, he had no idea, but damn it felt good.

Tonight would be a big one, he figured. They'd already kissed. Really that should have waited, but hey, they were adults. Date number two could have a lot more kissing.

He let out a long steady breath to calm his nerves. Closing his eyes, he sent up a little prayer for the night to go well, because he really—really—wanted it to go well.

As he turned down her street, Kent looked at his watch. It was seven-fifteen. He hated to be late, but he'd taken that damn tie off and changed one more time.

There was a beat-up red pickup truck out front of the house, which, when he thought of it, might have been there the night before. Oh, how could he remember anything such as a detail as that. All he could remember was kissing Bethany and hoping he was going to get to do a lot more of that tonight.

Kent put the car into park and opened the door just as the front door to the house opened and Bethany stepped out.

To say his breath was taken away, would be an understatement. The short dress seemed to fit her casual style. The bright color highlighted the flame of hair that cascaded over her shoulders. He was sure there was never a time she could possibly look bad.

He hurried around the to the other side of the car as she came toward him.

"I'm really sorry I'm late. My nephew was helping me pick out my outfit."

"No, you're fine."

He pulled open the door and she quickly slid past him and sat down. Not so much as a hug or a kiss. Something seemed to be bothering her. That was okay too. He just wanted to be with her.

Kent shut the door and walked around to the other side. "Is there any place you want to go?"

"Anywhere. Just go," she said.

Her arms were crossed and she kept her gaze out the front window. Kent looked back at the house assuming that

Susan would be running after her, but the door remained closed.

"Italian? I saw a..."

"That's fine."

Kent took a deep breath, started the car, and drove away from the house. It wasn't promising to be the romantic night he'd hoped for. Perhaps this was better, though. He'd either help her through whatever was eating at her, or he'd quickly realize there was a reason she was the one that was killed off in all her movies.

He drove through town until he found the restaurant he'd been thinking about when he passed it a few days ago. Usually, you couldn't go wrong with Italian. How many people could screw up a plate of spaghetti?

Kent parked his van in the parking lot and opened his door just as she did the same. There wouldn't be a grand chance to be a gentleman tonight, he thought.

Closing his door, he could hear her slam hers. He took a deep breath of caution and walked around the van with a smile.

"I've been dying for pasta."

Bethany turned to him and kissed him hard on the mouth. The action was so sporadic he tripped backward against the van and hit his head.

"Sorry," she said with a regretful look on her face.

"God, don't be sorry." He stood and rubbed the back of his head. "I just didn't expect that. Certainly didn't mind it either. What do you say we try that again?"

For the first time the slightest hint of a smile crossed her lips as she moved in and wrapped her arms around his neck.

"This is better," he said as he dipped his head and took over the kiss she'd started.

When their lips parted, he rested his forehead to hers. "Everything okay?"

"No. But we can discuss that over dinner. I'm sorry I was in such a mood."

"We all have them. I'm here to listen."

Kent took her hand, intertwining their fingers, and walked toward the front door of the restaurant.

Inside was quaint, cozy. The smell of garlic permeated the air. His stomach rumbled and Bethany turned with a grin.

"Hungry, Mr. Black?"

"Almost always."

"Me too."

Her mood seemed to have lifted after she'd kissed him. That had to be positive if he brought out the best in her.

They were seated in the corner. Red gingham tablecloths adorned each table. Tacky bottles of wine and statues of fat chefs holding pizza adorned the shelves on the walls.

"I don't even have to look at the menu. I want spaghetti with meatballs. A huge plate of it. And bread, lots of bread," Bethany said with wide eyes.

"You are hungry, aren't you?"

"Life is too short to starve. And I'm starving. I haven't eaten since yesterday sometime."

The waitress took their orders and brought them a basket of bread. Bethany had a piece in her hand and was slathering it with butter before he'd even noticed it was on the table.

"Can I venture into asking you what happened today?" he asked cautiously. "I took it you were upset when you left the house. But if you don't want to talk about it…"

"Susan fired me."

Kent sat back in his chair. "She fired you? Aren't you family?"

"Family can fire family."

"I suppose. But why?"

"I deserved it. I was late. I was a mess. I forgot things that were my responsibility to bring. I dropped a tray of food."

Reaching across the table he took her hands, which he'd noticed had begun to shake.

"Calm down."

"I can't. I ruined the luncheon for her. She had other jobs riding on that job. I can't take that back and make it better. I deserved to be fired. Only now I can't pay my rent."

"Susan doesn't come across as the kind of woman who holds a grudge. I'll bet if you talk to her, you two can work this out."

Bethany nodded. "I'm just a little worked up over it."

"Of course you are. Let's have a nice meal and I'll take you back early so you can talk to her about it."

She didn't agree to his proposition. Instead, she stood from her seat and walked around to his side of the table. Taking the seat next to him, she rested her hand on his knee, which managed to ramp up his heart rate to a dangerous level.

"How about I forget about my horrible day and stay with you for the night."

Kent swallowed hard and willed his body to behave as she touched him. "I…of course…don't you…" He stopped and took a breath because he sounded like an idiot. "Are you sure?"

"Absolutely sure," she said, lifting her hand into his hair and raking her fingers through it.

It was official, he thought as he placed his napkin on his lap. He was going to lose his mind over this woman. He could feel it slipping away every minute he was around her—and he liked it.

Chapter Fourteen

Kent sincerely thought it would be best to take Bethany back home after dinner. She'd had three large glasses of wine and had eaten all of her dinner, a few bites off of his, and most of the basket of bread. He certainly didn't mind. But looking at her in the van, her head rested against the back of the seat and her eyes closed, he thought it was taking advantage of the situation to take her to his hotel.

"Why don't I take you back to your place? Something tells me you could use a good night's sleep tonight."

She rolled her head so that she faced him and opened her eyes. "I don't want to go home."

"You need to talk to Susan."

"Not tonight. I don't want to talk to anyone but you tonight."

That should have been flattering, he supposed. However, looking at her he wasn't sure.

"How about I order us up a pot of coffee to the room when we get to the hotel? Maybe it'll make you feel better."

She only nodded and he was sure she'd then fallen asleep on the ride to the hotel.

Bethany opened her eyes when she felt the van stop. "This is your place?"

Kent chuckled. "Yeah. It's ugly, but they do have room service and an outdated gym."

She sat up and opened the door.

"Let me help you," he offered and she sat still, realizing she had eaten more than she had in months. Add the wine and she wondered why he hadn't just pushed her out of the car and onto Susan's lawn.

Kent hurried around the front of the van, then stood before her with his hand extended. She took it and he helped her out.

"I'm a mess, huh?"

"You just look a little lost, that's all. I know you had a rough day. But we'll get you some coffee and…"

"I wanted to have sex with you."

He cleared his throat and she could see the flush in his cheeks turning brighter. "That's quite an offer."

"I know. I'm a mess. You don't have to be nice to me tonight. I'll sober up a bit and get a cab."

"You're in good hands, sweetheart. Let's just get you upstairs."

She leaned against him. She couldn't believe she had just told him that she wanted to have sex with him. How embarrassing.

Suddenly that massive meal she'd consumed and the wine were mixing and she didn't feel good at all.

"Is there a bathroom in the lobby?"

"Yes." He pointed her in the right direction and she hurried toward the door.

Though she'd fully intended on ridding herself of the meal and the alcohol she'd consumed, she hadn't thought it would happen spontaneously.

She had barely reached the stall before she hurled her dinner into the toilet. Though she purged her meals often, she'd never get used the vial feeling that vomiting had on a body. She hadn't eaten all day and then to pig out as she had and to drink—she'd been asking for this. It was a punishment for her horrible attitude and behavior today. Susan never should have had to wait for her or work around her. The money she probably lost was—she didn't even want to think about it. Eric was probably livid with her too by now. Why wouldn't he be? She'd upset Susan so much she wouldn't blame them if they asked her to move out.

She'd be on her own again. She was used to that. Family had never been there for her anyway, why would now be…

Another wave of sickness moved over her and she heaved again and again before falling to the floor next to the toilet.

The sobs came next. They always came next, but this time it was because she was lying to herself. Her family had been there for her. Her father kept her safe and Eric had accepted her right away. Her sisters were working on a relationship with her and so were her brothers. Her mother was gone at her own hands. Bethany couldn't be blamed for her past.

The sobs came harder and she could hardly breathe.

Back in her bathroom there were pills to stop the vomiting. There were pills to keep her calm. She could sleep all night if she were just home.

"Bethany? Are you in here? Are you okay?"

Kent's voice echoed in the bathroom.

"You can't be in here. It's a ladies' room."

"You've been in here for twenty minutes. I told the manager I was coming in to get you."

She saw his feet under the door. He stopped right above her and pushed open the door.

"You need a doctor," he said looking down at her.

"I'm just a little sick. I'll be fine."

"C'mon, let me get you upstairs."

Though the thought of the pills back home seemed enticing, so did laying down on a soft bed.

Kent helped her from the floor and slowly they walked to the elevator. He kept his arm wrapped tightly around her waist.

As the elevator door closed, he could hear her sob.

"Are you okay?"

"No," she moaned. "You must think I'm a mess of a person. I'll understand that if you take me home tomorrow, you'll never want to see me again."

That's not what he wanted at all. Everyone was allowed bad days. So this one was a horrible one for her. He understood that. He'd had a million of them himself. God, when he thought back to the file drawer he had of rejection letters, it was a wonder he ever wrote another word.

"Let's get you feeling better. I can't imagine that I won't want to see you again. I happen to like you a lot."

"You do?" She stumbled against him as the elevator door opened.

"I do."

She was quiet the rest of the evening. He'd managed to get her into his bed, pull off her shoes, and cover her up. She hadn't gotten sick again and he was very grateful for that.

Kent had laid a cold, wet towel on her forehead and she'd drifted off to sleep. She may have thought she wanted sex with him, but that was very obviously not going to happen now.

Because his mother had raised him properly, he managed to find Susan's phone number and call her. He wanted her to know that Bethany was in good hands.

"Is she okay?" she asked.

"She's going to be. I just wanted you to know what happened and that I have her."

"I feel awful. I'm sure she was so worked up over today that it made her sick. I shouldn't have told her she was fired. I've dropped trays and been late before."

"I'm sure once you talk it out everything will be okay," he offered.

"I can bring over some clothes. Anything you need."

"I think she's fine. I'll call you if anything happens. I'm going to let her sleep it all off. I don't have to be anywhere tomorrow."

"Thanks, Kent."

He smiled as he watched her sleep peacefully. "It's all my pleasure."

Disconnecting the call, he set his phone on the table. A few moments later his alarm went off to call his nephew before bed.

He winced. There was no way he could read a bedtime story tonight. Quickly, he texted his sister.

I have company. Can't call.

She returned his text nearly immediately. *You got her to your room?*

He sighed. *Long story. Not so glamourous. Will call in the morning. Love you all. Goodnight.*

Bethany stirred as he set his phone back down.

Instinct had him move to her and kneel down next to the bed. "Can I get you anything?"

"Water."

"I can do that."

"A T-shirt."

He chuckled. "I can do that too." He stood and walked to the dresser where he pulled out his biggest T-shirt, to give her some comfort.

He walked back to the bed and sat down on the edge next to her. "I'll go down and get you a bottle of water. Here's the shirt."

Bethany moved the towel from her forehead. "Will you help me put it on? I promise not to jump you or anything," she said weakly.

He'd dreamed of touching her. In fact, he was very sure he knew what her skin would feel like under the tips of his fingers. This, however, wasn't how he imagined getting the opportunity.

As she tried to sit up, he moved to help her. The dress was bunched around her and he thought, as she inched it up, he might have a heart attack.

Kent helped pull the fabric from her pale skin and up over her head. Quickly he held up the T-shirt hoping to escape without his fingers touching her skin or his gaze getting stuck on her breasts and how they beautifully filled the delicate bra.

He swallowed hard as he slipped the T-shirt over her head and his fingers then brushed down her back as he eased the fabric on her.

The moment she was covered he stood.

"I'll go get that water."

Did he look to her to be as frightened as he felt, he wondered as he grabbed the room key card off the dresser and headed down the hall for a four dollar bottle of water.

The expense was nothing. The moment alone was priceless.

What had caused her to get so sick? He'd sure planned the night to end differently than it was. He worried about her, though. In two days, he had to leave Georgia for a week. The book tour couldn't be postponed.

Maybe she'd like to go with him. If she began to feel better, that would be an option.

He laughed at himself as the bottle of water dropped from the machine. Why would she want to travel with him? They didn't know each other at all, really. Just because he'd been just a little obsessed with her when he saw her, didn't mean she'd want to get to know him. No, it was a bad idea.

However, maybe it would help her out.

He picked up the water and headed back to the room.

From what he already knew about her she wasn't close to her father. Her mother had passed and her family was just coming into acceptance of her. Would it really matter that she left town with a man she didn't know very well? Would they actually notice she was gone?

It would give her and Susan some time apart. Maybe they could both cool off after their fight earlier that day.

He slipped his key into the door. When she felt better, he'd ask her.

She was asleep again when he walked into the room. Only now she was uncovered and the T-shirt had hiked up over her hip.

It might be worth calling the front desk to ask if they had another room. Having her in his bed, half naked, was going to drive him absolutely mad.

Chapter Fifteen

Bethany woke with a pounding headache. She sat up slowly and rested her head in her hands.

She'd made a mess of everything yesterday, including her date with Kent.

Kent.

When she looked around, he wasn't there. Had she scared him away? Forced him to leave his own hotel room?

With that in her head, she looked around for her dress, which he'd hung up in the closet. She pulled it from the hanger, stripped out of the T-shirt, and slipped on the dress.

After a quick glance in the mirror, she realized she looked as bad as she felt. Dark circles had formed under her sunken eyes. Her skin wasn't a normal color either.

A very deep seeded worry began to creep into her. She'd seen her mother's transformation from vibrant to dead. How could she possibly look like her mother had?

Turning on the water, she splashed her face to wash off the previous night. She swished water in her mouth to dilute the taste.

With her fingers, she attempted to settle the curls, opting to braid her hair instead.

One more look in the mirror and she realized nothing had helped. Who would want to cast her in any movie?

No one—and that was why she was in Georgia in the first place.

Bethany gathered her shoes in her hand and flung her purse over her shoulder just as the door opened and Kent walked through.

"You're up," he said with a smile that quickly faded. "And you're leaving."

"I thought I ran you off. I should just go home and get…"

His eyes narrowed. "Why don't you sit down for a few more minutes. I brought some coffee, some juice, bananas, muffins." He nodded to the paper bag he had in his arms. "Let's have some breakfast and then I'll give you a ride home."

Her stomach clenched at the very thought of food. But she knew she needed to eat. If she was going to break the chain of destruction her mother had programmed her with, she needed to start now.

Bethany set her purse down on the bed and followed Kent to the table where he set out a little buffet.

"I didn't know what you'd eat. I got a little of everything I thought would be okay for an upset stomach."

"I'm sorry about last night," she said reaching for a banana. "I hadn't eaten all day and I got carried away. And the wine…"

"You don't have to apologize to me." He picked up a muffin and began to peel back the wrapper. "I called Susan last night to tell her you were sick and that I was taking care of you."

Bethany bit into the banana and chewed slowly. "Did she even care?"

His brows narrowed together. "Of course she cared. Why wouldn't she?"

"I'm sorry," she rested her elbow on the table and her head in her palm. "I'm used to people throwing you to the curb when you mess up. When you're not perfect."

"I've never met a perfect person in my life."

"You didn't grow up under the scrutiny of Hollywood."

"Thank God." He set his muffin down. "Come on tour with me."

Bethany stared at him, the banana poised at her mouth for a bit. "Go with you?"

"I have four stops next week. Come with me."

"I don't…"

"You don't need to answer me right now. Well, by tomorrow you do." He winked. "But get away from here for a few days. Let the dust settle between you and Susan."

She took another bite of the banana and thought about what he was asking.

"You don't know me," she said.

"I can't think of a better way to get to know you."

Bethany sat back in the chair and studied him. His eyes were fixed on her—and she knew what she looked like. It didn't seem to bother him that she could easily be mistaken for a zombie.

Taking another bite of her banana, she thought about it.

"If I'm not working—I don't have anything. The Walkers might be well off enough, but I was never considered a…"

"I have enough to see us through. You'd be my guest." He reached across the table for her hand. "I can give Susan some money for the rent too. Whatever it would take to have you join me."

The tremble started from her toes and soon her entire body was shaking from nerves. This man *wanted* to spend time with her. He wanted to be alone with her and he had nothing to gain.

"I'm meeting my father for lunch today," she said as she remembered. "Would you mind if I gave you an answer tonight?"

Kent eased back in his seat. "That would be fine."

He took the lid off his coffee cup and blew the steam away as she finished the banana.

"And Bethany," he said raising the cup to his lips. "I won't be hurt if you say you won't go with me. I'd still like to see you when I get back. I think we might have a little something between us."

She bit down on her lip. "You'd come back to Georgia?"

"I'm finding I like it here quite a bit."

~*~

Susan wasn't home when Bethany walked through the door. Perhaps it was best. She'd have some time to get ready for her lunch with her father. It would also give her time to work on the apology she needed to give to Susan.

Bethany stepped into her shower and let the water wash off the night. It should have gone better than that, she thought. Kent shouldn't have seen her at her lowest, but he had. The more amazing part was he didn't seem put off by it.

She lathered shampoo into her hair and worked it around.

Thinking about his invitation, she realized no one had ever invited her to go away with them. She could still remember the look on her cousin Eric's face when she asked to stay the night on his couch. She was use to her presence being a nuisance.

Then she thought of Susan. She hadn't been a nuisance to her. She'd invited her to live with her having only known her for a few hours. They'd worked very well together until Bethany blew that.

She rinsed the shampoo from her hair, finished her shower, and stepped out. Wrapping the towel around her, she felt the hard reality of guilt land solidly in her stomach. It was a horrible feeling.

As she took another towel to wrap around her head, she noticed the bottles of pills still in her trash can from when she'd thrown them all there.

She wrapped the towel around her hair and looked down at them. They needed to stay there. She needed to carry them out to the trash can and say goodbye to them, but it was like seeing a part of her mother lay there in the trash.

Later. She'd deal with it later.

Right now she needed to get dressed for lunch with her father. If Susan happened to arrive before she left, she'd be ready to grovel.

Chapter Sixteen

Bethany felt right in her dress, pearls, heels, and makeup. Her hair flowed over her shoulders and the scent of her perfume lightened her mood. A little chain strap to the cute clutch hung over her shoulder. One thing she'd always enjoy, no matter if she were in Georgia or California, was a little glamour.

She could hear noise from the kitchen as she descended the staircase. It was calm noise, she decided. Not like the sound of pots and pans from the previous morning.

With care, Bethany slowly walked into the kitchen where Susan stood steeping a cup of tea as she scrolled through Facebook on her iPhone.

"Hello," she said softly and Susan raised her head and smiled.

"Hello. How are you feeling? Kent said you were sick."

Bethany forced her shoulders to ease, releasing the tension in her neck from her nerves.

"I was worked up. Too much wine. Too much pasta. I'm fine now."

"Good."

Bethany walked further into the kitchen. "I want to apologize for yesterday. I was a mess and I know I cost you more jobs and probably a great deal of money, which I can't make up either. You're very important to me and I'm sick over it all."

Susan set her phone on the counter and turned toward her. "It was like you weren't even you yesterday. I was really scared when I couldn't wake you up."

"I'm sorry."

Susan took a step toward her, gathered her hands in hers, and looked her right in the eye. "I know how your mother died, Bethany. Trust me. I checked you out before I let you move in."

Bethany could feel the air in her lungs begin to gather and it felt as though she were being choked.

"I need to know," Susan continued. "Are you taking drugs?"

The air released with a great force, causing her to suck in another breath, which she did choke on.

"You're accusing me?" she asked, her voice cracking.

"I'm asking. I've never seen anyone not wake up when someone touches them."

Bethany thought about that. She'd seen it—only when she'd touched her mother, she never, ever woke up.

"I had a restless night and I took a sleeping pill."

"Sleeping pills? Bethany…"

"I know. That's how she eventually died, but it's not like that. I don't take them every night. I don't take too many and I don't follow them down with vodka. It was only half of one too."

Susan pulled her in and held her tightly. "Please tell me you don't do that often. I'll stay up with you if you need me too. I'm so worried."

"There's nothing to worry about," she said pulling back. "I'm fine. Sleep is hard for me. I have nightmares. I left a lot of crap back in California and then I come out here only to be attacked by my mother's ex-lover. You don't just get to move on from all of that."

Tears rolled down Susan's cheeks. "I didn't think about all that. Douglas isn't going to hurt you anymore."

"I know that."

"What happened in California?"

Bethany's phone buzzed in her purse. She dug it out and looked at the text. "Dad is waiting for me."

"Bethany…"

"We'll talk later," she said tucking her phone back into her purse. "Are we okay?"

"Of course we are. And you can have your job back. I shouldn't have flown off the handle like that."

"Thanks," Bethany said with a smile. "I don't hold it against you. I deserved it." She turned to leave, but then turned back. "I guess, if I'm employed again, I'd better ask for some time off."

"Why?"

"Kent asked me to travel with him next week."

The tears had dried and Susan grinned. "So the two of you are really seeing each other?"

Bethany shrugged. "He took care of me last night and he didn't seem put out."

"He seems like a really genuine man."

"I think he is."

"Are you going with him then?"

"Should I?"

Susan laughed. "You'd better get going. Your dad is waiting."

Bethany nodded and left with a small wave. Things had been mended between her and Susan, but she still didn't have an answer as to whether she should go with Kent or not.

~*~

How come TV during the day was so lame, Kent wondered. He rested against the headboard, pillows stacked under him, and his computer on his lap.

The morning had been very productive when it came to getting some writing done. He'd plotted out the beginning of his next book, but he knew that was just clearing his mind. Even when he plotted out books, they never ended the way he'd planned. Characters had a way of telling the story themselves. He was just the channel they used to get their story told.

Now he was wasting time. The TV was usually never on when he worked, but today he wanted its distraction. He'd walked down to the coffee shop and ordered a pricey drink, which was now sitting on the table getting cold. Again, another attempt to avoid getting his writing done.

The truth was he wanted to call Bethany and check in on her. He wanted to see if she'd talked to Susan. He wondered how she was feeling. Simply put, he missed her.

Kent growled. He had a tendency to get a bit obsessive over things he found of interest. It started with a Rubik's Cube years ago. Once he'd learned to solve them then he had to have every kind. Then it was speed and competing. Next it was gaming. How many hours had he spent looking at a stupid TV, some days never seeing sunlight? Then it was golf and finally writing, which he obsessed over more than anything else in his life—well, that was until the day he met Bethany Waterbury.

Okay, it was new. He enjoyed her company. Craved her kisses. Loved the scent of her—well everything about her.

Sure, last night was disappointing. No one wants their date to be throwing up after dinner. Sooner or later every relationship has that day where they see each other sick. One of them steps up and takes care of the other. So that was the second date—or what he was considering their second date.

Kent poised his fingers over the keys on his computer. Obsession would be if he started digging for information on her. She was an actress—a famous actress. The Internet had to be full of things about her.

He typed in her name on a Google search and then stopped before entering.

She'd tell him anything he'd ever want to know. He was sure of that. All he'd have to do was ask and engage her in conversation.

His finger twitched over the enter key.

She was part of the Walker family. He could look them up. What harm would that do? It sounded as though they were a big name in the area. And the Walkers, Eric specifically, was related to Lydia, so he could look into her too. She was fascinating. He loved women who were entrepreneurs. What about Bethany's sister with the bridal store? He could look into her store.

Suddenly he had an entire day of Internet surfing planned and he didn't even have to actually look up Bethany Waterbury.

~*~

Bethany walked into the restaurant and scanned the tables for her father. The sophisticated man sat at a corner table. He'd donned a sports jacket and the large watch on his wrist caught the sun. His hair was whiter than she'd remembered and hadn't she only seen him a few weeks ago?

She realized she'd never really studied him, as she was doing now. He hadn't been prominent in her life and she'd never cared to really take the time to get to know him.

Well, that's what she was doing now. Getting to know him. Finding out who she was. Learning to be part of a family that embraced the very meaning. Falling in love.

That one caught her off guard as she let the words flow through her mind. Falling in love wasn't in her plans and she'd only just met Kent. How could she even possibly have let that into her conscience?

Bethany shook off the thought as her father looked up from his phone and toward the door. When he saw her he stood and moved to her.

"I thought you'd changed your mind," he said taking her hands and kissing both of her cheeks. "I'm glad you're here."

"Sorry. I've had a crazy week. I'm a little out of sorts and running late everywhere."

"You're just fine and you look beautiful."

"Thank you," she replied with a smile. She was grateful for the opportunity to get to know the man whose blood coursed through her body.

"You look so much like your mother," he added as he escorted them to the table. "She was so beautiful."

"You still think of her that way," she asked as he pulled a chair out for her and she sat down.

Her father took the seat next to her. "Of course I do. Why wouldn't I?"

"With all the things she did? Douglas Brant for one."

Her father nodded slowly, picked up his water glass, and took a sip. "We all have our shortcomings. It's very obvious I have my own." He set the glass down and clasped his hands together. "What she did doesn't belittle who you are. You are very beautiful. You are very talented. And I'm very happy you're here so I can get to know you. I didn't get the chance to do that before now."

"You never came around," she said bluntly as she picked up her own water and took a sip to soothe her throat. She was finding it hard to not be so curt with him.

"You're right. I was asked not to. And once I learned what a lunatic Douglas was, I didn't want you around either. For your own good. So much that did."

"You couldn't have known he'd attack me. Besides, Eric lost a lot more than I did. I didn't get shot. I didn't lose my business or my house."

"I know. He didn't deserve that." He rested his hand on hers. "I want to start with a clean slate, you and me. I've heard that you're staying in Georgia. Your sisters are enthusiastic about your plans."

"I am staying. I think family is what I need right now."

"Jake says you're seeing someone?"

Bethany stared at her father. "How would he know that?"

He smiled. "You may be working your way into the family, but the rest of them are solidly entwined. Word gets around fast."

She secured a solid smile and took a breath of courage. "I have gone out with Kent Black a few times."

Her father's eyes widened. "The author? They didn't tell me that part."

"He's just a normal guy. There is nothing any more special about his career than mine." She thought about that. "My old career that is."

"You're giving up acting?"

"I acted because it was expected from the daughter of Violet Waterbury. It's time to make my own path."

He patted her hand and then sat back in his chair. "I'm glad to hear that. I was as worried about you in California as I was having you come out here."

Bethany crossed her arms over her chest. "You worried about me. I'm sure you'll understand if I'm a bit defensive about that. Receiving a check on my birthday and Christmas wasn't really like having you around."

That got to him, she saw the flash of it in his eyes.

The waitress approached the table and took their order. Knowing she didn't care what was on her plate, Bethany ordered whatever her father had ordered.

When the waitress left, he looked up at her with his sad eyes. "I don't want that between us anymore. I'm here for you now."

Realizing it probably took a lot of effort for him to tell her that, she figured she should cut him some slack. After all, he'd invited her to lunch. He'd wanted to try to be part of her life.

"I'm sorry. I'd like to work on this relationship as well as the ones I'm starting with my sisters and my brothers. They all seem a little better equipped than I am at handling family matters. But I'll learn."

The worry faded from his eyes and a smile formed. "I'm very sorry about your mother's passing too. I should have reached out to you then."

He should have, but she was going to take the high road. "It was very sudden. I'm sure it would have been hard for you to get away."

Okay, she thought, that wasn't as nice as she'd have liked, but they were working on this relationship. One lunch was not going to fix it.

"I didn't realize she wasn't healthy," he said as he picked up his water again and sipped.

"When did you ever think she was?"

His eyes narrowed and focused on her. "I don't understand."

"You loved her enough to have a child with her. You'd have thought you'd have gotten to know her better."

"She was ill?"

Bethany's therapist said she'd go through different stages of mourning. One stage was anger and sitting there with her father she felt that stage erupt.

"She was a drug abuser, Dad," she said calling him 'Dad' for nearly the first time ever to his face. "Diet pills. Anti-depressant pills. Sleeping pills. You name it, she had a prescription for it. She drank vodka in a water bottle. She'd stay up for days and sleep for days. She threw up every meal she ever ate and went home with nearly every man who made any kind of pass at her. Yes, she was ill." Bethany picked up her water to take a sip and noticed how her hands shook. She set the water back down and clasped them in her lap as the waitress delivered their food. Too much of that hit too close to home.

"I didn't know," her father said weakly, looking down at his plate. "She always told me she had things under control."

"She lied—that was another thing she was good at. Nothing was under control."

Bethany wanted to eat, but she couldn't make herself. She pushed away her plate.

"You're not going to eat?" Her father looked up at her.

"If you don't mind, I'll take it home. I seem to be a little worked up."

He nodded and sat silent for a moment. "I didn't mean to bring this all out. I wanted some quality time with you."

She could argue with him or she could accept his gesture. "I think this all needs to be worked out. I've been here nearly three months and I've seen you a few times. You need to know how I grew up or my time here is as wasted as it was in California."

Her father took a bite of his lunch, wiped his mouth, and set his napkin back on his lap. When he looked at her she knew he was serious about wanting to be part of her life. There was a way about him that said he'd take it all back if he could. Whether he said it or not, she believed that he might.

"How is your living arrangement with Eric's fiancée?"

"Susan? She's very nice. Though she'll be leaving as soon as Eric's house is finished."

"It's almost done," he confirmed. "What will you do then?"

"I don't know. I'll have to talk to her about her plans with the townhouse. I suppose I could rent it. Take over her lease. I'd need a roommate."

"What about one of your sisters or brothers?"

She chuckled. "They have places to live." She gave it some thought. "I could ask Lydia. Something tells me if she had a place to go she wouldn't stay at her grandfather's anymore."

That made her father laugh. "I'm very surprised those two never bolted."

She knew the blood between the families was strained, but she'd leave that for another day.

Her father took another bite of his lunch. "What about the author? Do you think things are serious?"

She shrugged and pulled a french fry from her plate and ate it. "I don't know. He's very intriguing. I'd like to think he genuinely likes me."

"You doubt him?"

"He knew me from my movies."

"You think he has a fascination that isn't real?"

She reached for another fry. "Maybe."

"And did you read his books?"

"Only one. Under protest."

"And?"

She let out groan. "I liked it. I liked it a lot. I've downloaded the others to my Kindle."

He laughed. "Maybe it's just a mutual appreciation."

She liked that. Yes, that's what it was.

"He invited me to go to his next tour stops."

"And?"

"And I don't know. I don't know him, really. My luck with men is about as good as your luck with women."

He choked on his lunch and sipped his water. "Well, you are my daughter aren't you? Just say what you think."

"Sorry," she said hiding her smile behind her water glass.

"I know you can take care of yourself, so what are you afraid of?"

Bethany sat back in her chair. "What if I fall in love and come up short? What if I'm just like my mother and I drive him away?"

"And what if you're a very different person and you find true love? My brother found it. I have been jealous of that marriage from day one. I'll admit it. They love each other and stand by each other. But he had to make mistakes first."

"Eric's mother?"

"Yeah, but I think Eric turned out fine. Don't tell him I said that."

She laughed and pulled her plate closer. "You think I should go?"

"I think you should consider letting yourself actually feel what I think your heart has already felt."

"That's kinda deep, Dad."

"I gamble at everything. Even matters of the heart. But once in awhile, when you win—you're on top of the world."

That part Bethany understood. It was when you lost there was sure destruction. She'd seen that too. Would Kent hate her forever if she broke his heart?

A keen sense of loss had crept into her chest and squeezed as she left the restaurant.

Lunch should have been relaxing. It had been a moment to bond with her father, so why was she leaving feeling so weighed down?

She knew why and she didn't want to think about it. She didn't want to admit that every negative thing that had been said about her mother reflected on her.

Every muscle in her body was tense. Even her hair was weighing her down. She needed something. Something stirred in her that needed to be awakened. An energy burned in her core and even her breath became quickened.

Bethany hadn't even been thinking of where she was driving until she pulled up in front of Kent's hotel.

Maybe she just needed some company—some validation that she wasn't Violet Waterbury.

Chapter Seventeen

Pearl had run her bridal boutique for four years, Kent had learned. She'd won some award too, for a bridal design, or something. It didn't make sense to him.

The man Bethany had met at the coffee shop was her brother Jake. He was a mechanic during the day, but had quite a reputation as a race car driver. That was fascinating, he thought. He could always use that kind of information in a book.

Lydia seemed to be following in her mother's footsteps in real estate. Her mother owned the building where the *Garden Room* was located and Lydia was part owner of the restaurant they'd dined at the other night. Her father was military and had passed. Her grandfather was some wealthy landowner who also had oil rights.

A lot had been written on Byron Walker over the years, Kent found. He'd skipped over a few articles, just to not become too knowledgeable. It seemed as though there was a reason Bethany wasn't too close to him.

Eric Walker ran a horse boarding company which had been closed down earlier in the year when two horses died. A few weeks later his house had been set on fire and Eric had been shot.

Kent scooted the laptop closer to him and kept reading the article which had been published in a local paper.

Bethany had said that she and Eric were in the house when it caught fire, but she'd left out a key element. The house had been set on fire by Officer Douglas Brant after he'd shot Eric Walker and kidnapped Bethany Waterbury, daughter of Byron Walker.

Kent felt the hairs on the back of his neck stand up. Officer Douglas Brant had been arrested after he was treated at a local hospital for a gunshot wound inflicted by Ms. Waterbury upon her escape from her captor.

Kent ran his hands through his hair. This maniac had hurt her. He'd shot her cousin and kidnapped her.

His stomach churned. What else had he done to her in that time?

Kent was sick, but he needed more. He needed to know that Bethany Waterbury hadn't suffered at the hands of this man.

Blinking at the bottom of the screen was a link. Because of his searches, it had brought up other relevant topics.

The Death of actress Violet Waterbury.

Kent closed his laptop and rested his head against the headboard.

He wouldn't go there right now. Bethany could share that with him when she was ready. Right now he'd get a shower and then call her. Knowing what she'd been through, he had a desperate need to be with her, protect her, and love her.

Setting his computer on the table, he headed toward the bathroom to take his shower, but not before the tone chimed on his phone, alerting him to a text from his sister.

Call me now!

Panic ripped through him as he hit the contact icon and then her picture. One ring and she answered.

"Have you done your homework on this woman you're in love with?" His sister's voice shrieked through the phone.

"I have. What are you doing? Snooping?"

"I'm just surfing the Internet."

He couldn't accuse her of anything. He'd done that too.

"Kent, she was kidnapped."

He let out a breath and sat down on the edge of the bed. "I know. I read that."

"She didn't tell you?"

"She told me she was in the house when it caught fire."

"*Caught fire?*" Her voice rose in pitch again and he pulled the phone from his ear. "She was kidnapped. Her cousin was shot. That man set fire to the house. She shot that man! Her mother committed suicide—well overdosed, but… And…"

"Stop!" He stood. "Stop! You're making me crazy."

"Kent, this woman has a big past and you're swooning over her."

"Swooning?"

"Yes. Swooning. I know you. You're jumping in with both feet and you don't know her."

But he did, he thought as he sat back down on the bed. He knew her soul and all of this drama wasn't part of who she really was.

He thought about what his sister had said. "Her mother…"

"Drug addict, Kent. There's a lot of information on her. I thought you said you'd read this stuff."

"That's where I stopped," he admitted.

"Well, you'd better read it. She was a tart."

"Hey!" he shouted in defense—though he didn't know her.

"Seriously. She moved from person to person, place to place. Some of the articles are old enough to say *she and her young daughter.*" She let out an audible breath. "She was a prescription drug user and alcoholic, it says. *Violet Waterbury found dead from overdose of prescription sleeping pills. Daughter Bethany Waterbury discovered her mother's body after she neglected to show for a photo shoot.*"

Kent felt the sharp pain of grief pierce his chest. "She found her?"

"Yep."

"God, that's horrible."

"You need to figure out who this woman is," his sister said. Desperation filled her voice.

"She's a lost soul."

"And you're going to find her?"

"I think I have," he admitted. None of the facts that he'd learned about her should change how he felt.

"You're going to get hurt."

"She's hurt. What if I'm the person that makes it all better for her? What if…"

"What if you find her dead from some overdose?"

"That's not fair!"

"I'm just saying. Kent, you're good natured. You have a good heart. You're lonely."

"I'm not enjoying this attack on my character or hers," he argued with her. "Is this why you called?"

"You know that's not why. I worry about you."

He winced. He knew she did. "I won't let anything happen to me—or her."

"Mom wants to meet her. It's only a matter of time before dad finds this crap on the Internet and tells her about it."

"She'll freak out," he admitted.

"Yes, she will." There was a moment of silence before she spoke again. "You really care for her?"

"I know it's crazy, but I do."

"You're a good judge of character."

"Oh, I'm glad you said that. I was beginning to think you didn't trust me with the good sense God gave me."

Now she laughed. "Keep me posted, okay?"

"I will."

"I forgot to ask about last night. You said you had company."

Kent winced again. "Yeah. She stayed the night."

"Already an intimate relationship? You are lonely."

"No, actually it wasn't that at all. She got sick after dinner and I took care of her."

"Sick?"

"Too much wine with her dinner. She'd had a fight with her cousin's fiancée, who she works for. She was just overwhelmed and got sick."

"Kent, people get worked up all the time."

"Right and they get sick from it."

"You know—Hollywood is full of people with eating disorders."

He growled. "And just because she was an actress, she has one?"

"I'm just saying. Maybe that's what happened. If they eat a lot they purge."

"You're making me crazy. She does yoga and runs all the time. I don't think that…"

"That's an addiction too," she added.

"You're trying to get me to not like her and that's not going to work," he argued as he stood and walked to the bathroom. He hadn't argued with his sister in a long time and he was remembering that he didn't like it very much. She had to have that last word. She had to make her point.

"Just be mindful. If you love her then we will too."

"I didn't say I loved her."

"You didn't say you didn't. Just be careful."

"I will. I love you. Kiss the rugrats for me."

"I will. Call me later, okay?"

He agreed and said goodbye then turned the shower on hot. His muscles were tense now and his mood had been shot. There had been a reason he hadn't clicked on the link that discussed Violet Waterbury's death. Now he wished he hadn't made the phone call either.

Kent pulled off his shirt and unbuttoned his pants just as there was a knock at the door.

Timing sucked, he thought and he headed to the bathroom. Whoever it was could just wait.

Just as he shut the door, he heard the knocking intensify. And he was fairly sure he heard a woman's voice call his name.

He let out a groan, walked to the door, and pulled it open.

Kent hadn't completely registered that it was Bethany before she pushed her way in and against him. Her mouth was quickly on his, hot and needing.

He kicked the door closed as he spun her against it.

Her fingers were on his chest and he was sure he might have a heart attack with her touching his bare skin. Oh, it would so be worth it, he thought as her nails dug into his skin.

Bethany laced her arms around his neck as he hoisted her up. She wrapped her legs around him and the pressed their bodies even closer together.

He could die happy and he hadn't even touched her.

"What are you doing here?" he managed between breaths before their mouths consumed each other's again.

"Need—you," she said, her breath labored as she took him under with another kiss that had his knees going weak.

A moment later she lifted her head. "Who's in your shower?"

"Me."

A laugh escaped her breathlessly. "You're here."

"Was getting in," he tried to focus now on the conversation while he still had her wrapped around him.

She wiggled from his arms and looked toward the bathroom. "You're alone?"

"Of course," his voice cracked.

"Good," she said as she pulled the dress off of her body and let it fall to the floor.

The blood quickly drained from his head and he leaned against the wall just to hold himself up. She stood before him in a matching set of pink lacy bra and panties. Yep, this is exactly how his fantasies of her had begun.

"I'm joining you," she said as she unclasped the bra and dropped it atop the dress.

He forced himself to breathe as she winked at him and disappeared into the bathroom.

Chapter Eighteen

Kent rolled over on his back and panted. His body was slickened with sweat and his hair showed the obvious trailing where Bethany had run her fingers through.

She rolled to her side and twirled the small tuft of hair on his chest around her finger. Did she know this was what she needed when she left the restaurant? Or had she caused a rip in the nice, calm relationship they were building?

"What are you thinking?" Kent asked, his breathing still labored.

"Are you sorry we…"

"Are you really going to ask me that after the shower, the counter, the floor, the bed, the chair, the bed…"

"Okay," she laughed. "I guess not."

Kent rolled to face her. "Are you sorry?"

"No. I'm not sorry. I'm scared."

He pushed at her hair, tucking it behind her ear. "Why are you scared?"

"This is where it ends. This is the point that I don't know how to have a relationship."

He narrowed his gaze on her and traced his finger over her shoulder. "Your relationships end with sex? Isn't that when they're supposed to get serious?"

She watched his eyes. They didn't hold judgment and neither had his words. Seriously, wouldn't a man usually get upset when he considered the woman in his bed having been with other men?

"I come from a place where sex isn't based on relationships of the heart. They're deal makers."

Now there was the shift in his gaze. "So there is no chance in assuming sex is love?"

"Right," she agreed as he sat up.

"Did you come here to make a deal?"

Bethany sat up next to him, pulling the sheet up around her to cover her naked body as if she were now ashamed.

"I came here because…well, I just…" She didn't know why she'd come. She'd just driven there because she was feeling so empty. She'd needed someone to validate—well, her. "I just seemed to drive here. I wanted to be with you."

A small grin formed on his lips. "You wanted to be with me?"

"Yes."

"I just happened to be half naked when you got here."

The seriousness of the moment seemed to fade away. "Yes. Honestly, I hadn't anticipated climbing in the shower with you."

Kent moved swiftly, rolling her onto her back and pinning her down with his body. "I've never been so happy to see someone in my life. My showers will never be the same."

Looking up at him she realized he didn't understand where things were headed.

"I don't expect anything from you, by the way."

The grin slipped away. "As in?"

"You don't have to come back to Georgia after your tour. You don't have to keep me around. When they cast your movie, you don't have to ask them to use me."

He rolled away, only this time he stood and found his towel, wrapping it around his waist. "You want me to ask them to cast you?"

"No!" She wrapped the sheet around herself and stood. "That's what I'm saying. I'm not asking for any favors. I'm not here to make or close any deals. Not with you."

His eyes widened. "Not with me?"

The warmth that their lovemaking had filled her with subsided and now her stomach was filled with sharp pains.

This wasn't something she wanted to discuss with him. She moved toward the bathroom where her clothes lay in a pile on the floor. Quickly, she scooped them up and headed for the bedroom to change.

Kent reached for her and spun her toward him.

A moment later his arms were wrapped around her and she was pressed against his chest. "I have a feeling we have a lot to talk about. I also have a feeling you're trying to run away from me and use this as an excuse for a relationship not to work."

"I...why would..." her stomach churned. "I'm going to be sick."

He let loose of her and she ran to the bathroom, slamming the door behind her. The few bites of her lunch she'd consumed came back and she hurled into the toilet.

"Bethany, are you okay?" he called from beyond the door.

"I'm fine. Go away."

"Never going to happen," he said as he pushed open the door and handed her a towel. "What can I get you?"

She could only stare at him. He was still there. They were done having sex. She'd been sick in front of him more than once now and there he stood with a towel, offering her assistance.

"I'm fine. I'll be out in a moment."

He nodded and backed out of the bathroom.

Kent pulled on his clothes and paced the room as he waited for Bethany to clean up and come out. His sister's words kept replaying in his head and he found himself cursing her for the phone call that now had him doubting Bethany.

When he heard the door open, he turned to watch her.

"I'm sorry about all this. I should get home," she said.

"Then I'll go with you."

Bethany shook her head. "No. I'll be fine."

He moved to her. "I'm not just going to give up on you, whatever you're thinking. I'm not a Hollywood, deal maker. I'm not anyone you've ever been with before."

She batted her eyes which had become moist with tears. "I'm not good for you."

"You get to decide that?"

Her mouth opened as she stared at him. "Kent, I'm damaged goods. This was nice, but…"

He moved in and kissed her hard on the mouth. Pressing his forehead to hers he held on to her tight. "Don't leave me and say this was nice. It is nice. You're not your mother. You're not damaged goods."

She pulled back slowly. "What do you know about my mother."

"It's out there, honey. I know you found her."

"You know she overdosed?"

He nodded and pulled back. "I know."

Tears streamed down her cheeks. "I've been with…"

"Shhh. It doesn't define you. I've been with two other women."

He should have been offended when she laughed and wiped her tears.

"Two?"

"Why is that funny?"

"Because you're famous and handsome."

"I am? Handsome, I mean."

"Sexy as hell," she moved to him and rested her hands on his chest. "I've been with more than two."

"Do you want to talk about that?" he asked, hoping that this wasn't the time she'd want to, but he'd listen.

"No. I don't ever want to talk about that."

And that told him they'd need to, but he was happy to have a reprieve from it for tonight.

"Are you going to go on my tour with me next week."

She bit down on her bottom lip. "I've been trying to decide. My excuse for not knowing you well enough isn't valid anymore."

He chuckled. "No, I'd say we know each other very well now."

"I'm not ready for the same thing to happen that happened at the signing the other day."

"You don't want anyone to recognize you?"

"It's your moment. Not mine."

"If you're with me, it's because I want you there."

"Are you sure?"

"I've never been more sure about anything."

Bethany took his hands and interlaced their fingers. She took a big breath. "I come with a lot of baggage. I'm going to tell you upfront that I will never blame you for leaving me."

"I don't think I'm going anywhere."

"You will, but let's see how far this goes. I'd love to go with you next week."

It was supposed to be a positive statement, he thought, but still she had entangled imminent doom into their relationship. He was just going to have to prove to her that he was willing to commit to forever. Saying the words, however, would have her running for the door.

He'd take it one step at a time. Maybe if Violet Waterbury had the right man, she'd be alive to support her daughter too.

Chapter Nineteen

Bethany had somehow convinced Kent to let her go home alone around ten o'clock. Of course that was after dinner. Room service for dessert. And, well, there had been another two hours of making love.

She sighed as she pulled her hair up into a ponytail and gave herself one last look in the mirror. Her cheeks were full and pink. Her eyes were bright. There was a tingling in her belly, but not the kind that made her sick.

Perhaps this was love. Maybe. She wasn't going to think more than that. Love never lasted forever and she wanted this to last as long as possible.

The trash can caught her attention. Inside were still the bottles of pills, right where she'd left them. Letting out a deep and thoughtful breath, she decided that was exactly where they still belonged. She was going through today with only happy thoughts of Kent. If she needed a dose of anything, it was him.

Her heart fluttered in her chest at the very thought of it. Now she couldn't wait to leave and go on tour with him. Just him and her for days in a hotel room. That sounded like heaven.

The next morning, she jogged down the stairs and out the front door for her first run in days. No more sleeping pills, she swore to herself. No more diet pills. No more binge and purge. She wasn't her mother and she had a man who cared about her.

The morning was still cool enough that she ran further than she'd anticipated. She found herself miles away at the coffee shop she'd met her brother at the other day and where she and Kent had exchanged glances.

The thought brought a smile to her lips.

Maybe she'd go in and get a smoothie. She could walk back to the house and enjoy her drink along the way. For the first time in a long time she wanted to just enjoy the morning. Every sight, sound, and smell seemed important today.

Pulling the earbuds from her ears, she walked through the front door, and stood in line. They certainly had a variety, she thought.

"You're up early," a man said from behind her.

Bethany cautiously looked over her shoulder to see her cousin Dane standing there. "Thought I'd go for a run. Just happened to run farther than I'd planned to."

"Is someone picking you up?"

She chuckled. "No. I just thought I'd get a drink and walk home. What are you doing in town?"

He shrugged. "Mom wants to go to breakfast and then go shopping for new shirts. She seems to think that moving to a new city means I need new clothes."

She nodded, remembering he had a job in Ohio. "That's right. When do you leave?"

"Four days. Mom's having a small dinner for me. Will you be there?"

"Oh, I think I'll be out of town."

"That's okay. With all the fuss over Eric's wedding, I'm sure I'll be in town a lot. Lydia said the dresses Susan picked out for all of you are beautiful."

"They are." She stepped forward in the line. "When did you talk to Lydia?"

"She's been out at Eric's barn lately. She has a horse out there."

"I didn't know that."

"New acquisition," he said as they stepped up further in line.

"Why isn't she keeping it at her grandfather's? There's ample room there."

Dane laughed. "I'm sure it's just to piss her grandfather off. What's worse than paying a Walker to do something you could do for free on Morgan land?"

"I suppose you're right." They approached the counter and ordered their drinks, then moved to the cashier. As she began to pull out the few dollars she'd tucked into her armband, Dane placed his hand on her arm.

"I'll get your drink."

"You don't have to do that."

"I'd like to."

Dane paid and made small talk with the girl behind the counter. She watched him smile at her and the girl laughed in return. He had a way with people, which was probably what made him successful in his career. But there was a shy side to him. He might be good with people, but Bethany was sure he'd prefer to not be around them at all.

He picked up the drinks when they were placed on the counter and handed hers to her.

"Thank you."

"My pleasure. Can I give you a ride home?"

Bethany shook her head and rested her hand on her cousin's arm. "No, but thank you. I'm looking forward to the walk."

"Eric's okay with you being out on your own?"

She pursed her lips. "Douglas Brant is locked up. He won't hurt me again."

"Right. I'm sure he still worries though."

"Like an overprotective father." She sipped her drink and let out a grateful sigh. "This is good. I suppose I should head back. Have a safe trip and I look forward to seeing you when you're home."

She leaned in and hugged him.

"Thanks. I'll see you around."

With a small wave, she left the store and headed back home.

The air was filled with so many scents. Flowers in bloom. The smell of freshly cut grass. She could hear the sound of kids in a nearby park and a fire engine a few blocks away.

These sights, smells, and sounds had been in Hollywood too, only she'd been too numb to notice.

Bethany sipped her smoothie.

In her mind, her troubles had only started when her mother died. But in this very peaceful moment, she needed to be honest with herself. They had started a long time ago.

She bit down on her lip, slowed her walk, and focused on herself.

When was the first time she'd sipped from her mother's coffee mug and spit it out? She was nine and it was pure vodka.

By the time she was thirteen she'd been suspended for showing up to school drunk and by fifteen for smoking pot in the girl's bathroom.

Her hands began to shake. She lifted her drink to her lips and took a slow, thoughtful sip to clear her head. This was a good moment to have with herself, she thought. She needed to embrace who she'd been. She'd dumped all this information on Pearl a few days earlier and now here she was, actually processing it in her own head.

Nearly every meal she'd eaten since she was fifteen had been thought out. She'd eat healthy for a few days, weeks even, and then she'd binge until she got sick and threw it all up. She'd lost her virginity that year too. That was too young. He was too old.

That left a vile taste in her mouth and she sipped her drink again hoping to wash it away. But she knew it couldn't fix anything. That man had been only the first in a long line of men who used her and whom she used. In fact, Kent was the first man she'd made love to—ever. The true meaning of the words themselves were now understood because she'd done them with someone she loved.

There was a bench a few feet in front of her. She quickly walked to it and sat down as her head had begun to spin. She'd been processing her past only to have the full realization of her future interrupt her.

She was in love with Kent Black.

She'd denied herself that thought earlier that morning. Love never lasted, she tried to remind herself, but suddenly she didn't believe that.

After all, hadn't she left everything behind for a new start—which meant a new mindset?

She sipped her drink again, but then stopped. She'd left the town—the state—but she hadn't left it all behind.

She'd lost her job with Susan because she'd overslept. Excusable if you'd had a late night reading some book, she thought with a grin. It wasn't acceptable, however, when you took a damn pill to escape any reality you just weren't ready to face.

She'd watched the lines form on her mother's face over the years. She'd seen her hair begin to fall out. Her teeth lose their sheen.

Bethany's heart began to race and pound against her ribs uncomfortably. Her mother drank until she couldn't function, then she'd taken sleeping pills to rest. She hadn't woken up. She—didn't—wake—up!

Suddenly her throat was closing and she could hardly breathe.

Looking around, she thought of where she was in relation to Pearl's store. She needed to get to her sister. Bethany didn't want to be this person anymore. She didn't want to die in her bed and miss out on anything.

She threw the smoothie in the trash and began to run.

A few minutes later and a few wrong turns, she was in front of her sister's bridal shop, looking through the front window. A beautiful bride spun in front of a mirror and her sister pinned up the bottom of the dress.

This wasn't a good time, and she quickly tried to clear her head. Pearl didn't need her in the way right now.

"Hey, what are you doing walking around?"

Bethany spun around when she heard Kent's voice behind her.

He looked at her and took hold of her shoulders. "What's wrong? You're as white as a ghost."

No…no…this wasn't good. He couldn't see her at a low time, not again.

"I, well, I just…" She closed her eyes and tried to find that courage from earlier. She wanted to be brave enough to share things with him.

Slowly she opened her eyes and looked at him. "I love you."

Now his eyes widened. "Oh. Oh! Wow! I wasn't expecting that."

"You shouldn't love me, though. You should go. You should go on your trip. You should move away."

He was shaking his head. "I don't understand. Did you just rob a bank or something? What's going on?"

"Bethany?" Her sister's voice came from the door and she turned to see her standing there. "What's wrong? Why didn't you come in?"

There was a throbbing in her ears now. A full blown panic attack had taken over and now that fluttery feeling she'd had in the pit of her stomach, which she'd called love, was heavy and painful.

"I'd wanted to talk. You're busy. I'll come later."

Pearl let the door to the store close behind her and walked toward Bethany. Her face had gone cold and that furthered Bethany's panic.

"I told you I'd always drop everything if I had to for you. You don't look well. You need a hospital."

That only angered her. "I do not. I'm fine," she said through gritted teeth.

"I'll take her home and get her some rest," Kent offered.

"I said I'm fine!" Any self-pity was gone and now she was only angry. "I had a moment. That's all. I didn't want to bother you," she said to her sister.

Pearl crossed her arms in front of her. "I've been reading up on all of this. This isn't real anger. You're lashing out to act like you're in control."

"I am in control!"

Kent held his hands up in surrender. "In control of what?"

Pearl simply shifted her gaze to Bethany, who now fumed at the scene this was causing.

"Nothing," she said.

"Wait. You just told me you loved me. Were you making that up?"

Bethany felt deflated. "No. I wasn't making that up."

"Good. Because I'm pretty sure I'm in love with you too. Not pretty sure, I mean I know I'm in love with you. My sister told me I'm in love with you and…" He stopped. "I ramble when I'm nervous," he admitted.

"I'd never say something like that to someone if I didn't mean it. I've never said it to anyone before."

"That's quite a compliment. Okay, then, if I'm that important, then tell me, what is all this about?"

Bethany clenched her jaw and looked at her sister. Pearl's stance softened and in that moment they exchanged feelings which corresponded to words that only sisters could understand.

Pearl gave her a nod and looked at Kent.

"My little sister is very courageous. She's dealing with a lot of crap and she was kind enough to confide in me."

"What crap? What's going on?" Kent pleaded with both of them.

Bethany reached for his hand as Pearl took a breath to speak. "Her mother died of a prescription drug overdose."

"I know."

"Bethany is a little too familiar with those prescription meds too. As well as having an eating disorder," her sister said as Bethany gripped tightly to Kent's hand and looked at the ground.

"Is that true?" he asked and she lifted her head slightly and nodded. "Okay, then." He let out a breath, but he didn't let go of her hand. "That's a lot to deal with. We need to get you some help."

"She's seeing a counselor," Pearl offered. "After she was attacked with Eric, everyone thought it was best."

"Good. It's good to get help when you need it." He pulled her to him and wrapped his arms around her. "Why don't I give you a ride home? We can talk about this and you can let me in on it."

Bethany raised her head fully and stared at him. His eyes were warm and kind. This didn't seem to ruffle him at all. "You're not mad?"

"Mad? Why would I be mad?"

Bethany shrugged.

Kent cupped her face in his hands. "I happened to fall in love with a woman who's seen a lot. I think we're a good team though and I think if we stick together we can beat this."

"You want to stay?"

"Honey, I don't have any intentions of going anywhere. I told you that. Yes, I want to stay. And as hard as it might be, I want to know everything about you."

"It's not pretty. I'm not a..."

"You're perfect," he interrupted. "The past is there for a reason, because it's past. We're moving into the future." He took her hand. "C'mon, I'll take you home."

Bethany nodded and smiled. She turned to hug her sister. "Thank you. I'm sorry I interrupted your day."

"Never—ever be sorry." She kissed her on the cheek. Then Pearl pulled Kent in close and hugged him. Bethany could hear her whisper in his ear. "Thank you. She means a lot to me."

That ache that had been piercing in her chest softened. Family—no matter what they were there for one another.

Chapter Twenty

Bethany was quiet on the ride home and Kent was okay with that. He needed a few minutes to wrap his head around what he'd just learned.

It made a lot of sense, though. She was hot and cold with her emotions. He'd seen her get sick after she ate though he'd never have imagined that was the problem.

Then his sister's words hit him right in the chest. She had warned him of everything he was now facing. Drugs. Eating disorders. A past he knew nothing about.

His hands grew damp against the steering wheel. He didn't really want to believe any of it. He wanted her to be normal—perfectly normal.

Well, hell, that wasn't fair either, he decided as he turned down her street. Who the hell was normal anymore? He lived out of hotel rooms and wrote about non-existent aliens in galaxies that didn't exist. Who was he to judge someone's reality? Maybe she found his shortcomings unattractive, which he didn't think she was. But his job was to help her. There was no reason to think it was a desperate problem— no, that was wrong. He needed to treat it as though it were desperate and nip it in the bud. She needed to be free of her demons and able to move forward in her life. She deserved that.

Kent pulled up in front of the house and turned off the van. "Looks empty."

"They're out at the house, I think. My dad says it's almost done."

Kent nodded and opened the door. "I'd like to see it."

"Really?" she asked as she climbed out of the van.

He stepped around the van and walked toward her. "Yeah. I've been in Georgia a few weeks and haven't seen anything but the city, really."

"Maybe later we can drive out there. You can see Eric's parents' home, what they're rebuilding, and his barn where he works."

"I think that would be very nice," he said, slipping his arm around her.

The small conversation had put her at ease. His interest in her family had sparked a little light in her eyes. They could do this. They could make this all right, he thought.

Bethany opened the door to the house. Scents of something Susan had baked that morning still permeated the air.

"I could get used to a house smelling like this," Kent said.

"It's new to me. My mother never—ever—baked anything. I'm lucky I know how to heat soup in a cup."

"I have a pretty good background in cooking. My mom thought I should know. I separate my laundry too. Who wants pink tighty-whities?"

She chuckled. "Maybe I'll learn someday to be domestically apt."

Kent shrugged and pulled her near. "Not a skill I'm totally sold on in a woman."

"Really? What man says that?"

"This one," he said tipping her chin up with his finger and pressing his lips to hers.

She let herself sink into him. After her meltdown at her sister's shop, she hadn't really expected him to be so calm and understanding.

He eased back and kept her close. "So, we have a lot of talking to do and you have some packing to do."

"Packing?"

"We leave tomorrow night and head for South Carolina."

"You still want to take me?"

"There has never been any doubt. But, in fairness to us both, you need to tell me everything—and I mean everything about you. You can't leave one ugly stone unturned."

She stepped back from him. "I don't like that idea at all."

"I'm not asking to shame you. I'm asking so I know where you're headed and what I can do to make sure you're headed there with me."

"You think like that?"

"I do." He stepped to her, taking her hands. "It appeared to me, that you reaching out to your sister said you wanted help banishing the demons in your past."

She couldn't find words to answer. All she could do was nod.

"That's what I thought. Let's get you healthy, Bethany. You're not your mother. You're a fine example of a bright and beautiful woman who has a lifetime ahead of her. I plan to be there for it, so let's make you healthy."

Bethany's breath became heavy and hard to push through her lungs. "You won't change your mind about me?"

Kent cupped her face in his hands. "I promise. Nothing can change my mind if you promise to tell me everything."

She gave it a moment's thought and agreed.

"Good. Where should we go to talk?"

"My room."

His brows drew together and he narrowed his gaze on her. "That sounds like you're avoiding us talking."

She laughed and shook her head. "When you see it, you'll understand."

She took his hand and led him up the stairs to her very own sanctuary.

She'd been right. Kent stood in the doorway and was in awe of the space. "You have a patio, and a king size bed in here."

"And my own bathroom with a Jacuzzi tub."

"So Susan's room is twice this size?"

Bethany shook her head. "Not even close."

"Why are you so lucky?"

She shrugged. "She said that it was easier to rent."

"Sure…sure. I get that, but damn!"

That made her laugh and she turned and pulled him into the room by gripping the front of his shirt. A moment later her mouth was on his and that sense that he could lose control with her, again, began to take over. But they had business. Unfortunately, he was going to have to be the bad guy.

He pulled back and let out a breath. "So where do you want to talk?"

Bethany let out a grunt. "I don't want to talk."

He gave her that eye he'd seen his own sister give her children. It must not have worked, because it only made her laugh.

"Fine. Let's go out on the patio. It'll give you a platform to jump from after I tell you everything."

"I'm walking out the front door—with you," he said to ensure her that he wasn't going to walk out.

"You're a very good man."

"I'm decent enough. And I meant it, I love you, no matter how crazy fast it's come about. I'm not going anywhere, Bethany."

For a moment she only watched him. He supposed it was to make sure he wasn't going to run—which he had no intention of doing.

She took his hand and led him out to the quaint little patio that overlooked the small back yard.

"This is nice."

"I do my yoga out here. It regenerates me," she said sitting down in the lounge and kicking her feet up on it.

It was the only place to sit, so Kent sat down next to her, turned so he could face her.

"Why do you do yoga?" he asked.

"My mind shuts off, for the most part. It just makes me feel good."

"I like that. Maybe you can show me someday. I can't even touch my toes."

"Liar."

"No, really. Loafers are the best shoes. I look good and I don't have to bend over and tie them."

She laughed again and concluded it with a sigh. Then her eyes met his and locked. "I do it because it's the only thing I can actually control. For a few minutes I can be one with the universe and I don't have to think about anything else."

"Why do you run so much?"

She chuckled slightly and looked away. "It keeps me thin."

"You look amazing."

Bethany shook her head. "The last director I worked with told me I was a cow. He even mooed at me."

He could feel the heat climb up in neck. "Are you kidding me? You have the most voluptuous body of any woman I've ever seen. Not to mention your eyes are mesmerizing and that hair..." He ran his fingers over it, giving her ponytail a tug. "Your beauty is hypnotic."

"You love me. It's different."

"It shouldn't be."

She kept her eyes locked on his. He didn't blink—he didn't look away. "Anyway. I run to stay in shape. I do yoga to clear my mind and to also stay in shape."

"To an excess."

She finally looked away. "I suppose I do."

Kent took her hands in his. "Let's talk about your eating disorder."

She groaned. "Another habit to keep cow comments at bay. It was also taught to me by my mother."

"Why does a mother teach her daughter something like that?"

She laughed aloud. "Oh, Lord, you'd be surprised what kids I knew were taught by their parents. You do realize where I was raised, right?"

"I just don't understand it. I was raised in a Christian home. We went to church. We played in the yard. Kissed girls behind trees on the playground. I was on a soccer team. I tried my hand at drama in school and I sang in the choir. I don't understand that this wasn't the norm."

Her face grew sad and as she blinked he was sure he saw the first of what would be many tears disappear.

"When I was six, I came to Georgia to meet my father. I remember Pearl was twelve. She'd just started wearing makeup and I thought she was everything. Audrey was fifteen and not very fond of me. I don't blame her, but she wasn't. But I remember they had a rope swing in the backyard. One of those with a knot in it holding a piece of wood. Pearl swung me on that swing. When they say go to your happy place, that's where I go. Back to that swing at my dad's house with my sister."

She swallowed and now wiped her cheek as another tear escaped before she continued.

"See, when I went back home with my mom, I went back to a one-bedroom apartment. I slept on the couch. Mom would leave me home at night and I'd sit in the bathroom, in the bathtub, with the door locked."

"Your mother left you alone at six?"

Bethany nodded. "She had *things* to do."

"Honey, that's not okay."

She nodded. "It was my norm. When I started school I got up and went. I came home alone. Sometimes she'd come home. Sometimes she wouldn't."

Kent felt his throat closing off the air in his lungs. No one deserved this kind of childhood.

Bethany reached to the back of her head and pulled the band from her hair. She looped it around her fingers and stretched it. "I watched her take a pill for this and a pill for that over the years. I never thought anything of it. I had a hundred uncles."

That part made Kent force down the vile taste of vomit he could feel pushing up.

She looped the band over her wrist and ran her fingers through her long, red curls. "She'd bring home a new guy every few months. They were wannabe producers and directors. They were all going to make her a big star. That didn't happen."

"I thought your mom had been in a lot of movies."

"Fourteen and a half."

"A half?"

"They fired her half way through one and recast her. She was too stoned, too drunk, or too MIA."

He nodded. "But you followed in her footsteps?"

"It was all I knew." She reached for his hands and interlaced their fingers. "When I was fifteen there was a director who wanted me in his film. Pretty exciting for a girl that no one had ever paid attention to."

"Lucky break?"

"Sure. Once I let him have my virginity and see what there was for me to offer him, I got the part."

Her fingers had tightened around his and he realized that she was holding on for dear life.

"Bethany…"

"Don't feel sorry for me, okay?"

"I can't help it."

"This only gets worse and if you want to know my life up to this point, then you have a lot of listening to do."

Kent nodded and sucked in a breath. He didn't want to hear another word, but he knew that didn't take away what had happened to her. So he braced himself.

He sat there on the lounge while she squeezed his fingers until they were nearly numb. For the next hour, she told him about the men she'd been with, all offering her opportunities for a night. There were drugs in high school. Alcohol suspensions in junior high school. For a short time, she had her say in Hollywood among the B-film community. She was wanted.

Food was a curse since she was fifteen and she binged and purged almost all the time. Though she felt she had that under control, or so she said.

Alcohol didn't seem to be a problem. That was something he was happy to hear, but the pills, she admitted, that had been something new since her mother had passed.

"I couldn't deal with it all. So I took all her pills and I started to look them up online. When things got too stressed I'd pick out the right pill. Then when Douglas attacked us…"

"You turned to them more."

"Do you blame me?"

"Not in the least." Now he pulled her close and held her next to his rapidly beating heart. "It's never going to be like that again," he promised.

"You're right. I'm never going back."

· "That doesn't matter. If you want to be rid of all this, then it should be. I'm here to see you through it. I'll get you help. I'll help you. Whatever you want, I'm here and I know your family is too. Pearl loves you and she wants what's best for you. I've seen Eric around you and I'm sure he's on my side too. He's on your side."

"That's why I stayed in Georgia. I didn't want to be someone who was found dead weeks later because no one missed them."

"It'll never happen that way."

"Promise?"

"With my life."

Bethany let go of his hand for the first time in nearly an hour. She stood from the lounge and reached for him.

"Follow me."

She led him to the bedroom. He figured she was going to want to seal the deal and he had to admit, after a roller coaster of emotions, he'd much rather take a roll in the sheets.

But she kept walking. She took him into the bathroom and stopped next to the sink.

"What are we doing?" he asked.

She pointed to the trash can and Kent gasped. "What are those?"

"Those are my mother's pills. The ones I've been using. The ones that killed her. I threw them away the other day after Susan fired me. See, I had all intention of making them go away."

He nodded and looked at the trash can that was nearly overflowing. "This is all of them?"

She opened the cabinet behind the mirror. "Yes. See, I took them all out."

Knowing she needed his help to make them disappear, he picked up the trash can and held it in his arms.

"Are you okay for an hour?"

"Why?"

"I want you to start packing for our trip. I'm going to take these and dispose of them. Far away from here, okay?"

She nodded. "We could just flush…"

"Nope. I'm going to make them disappear and you're going to let me."

"O-kay." She let out a short breath. "You're not leaving forever though, right? You're coming back."

"Of course I am."

"I told you a lot of horrible things."

He bent and kissed her forehead. "You did. You know what? It doesn't change anything. And guess what, you're only twenty-four years old. That leaves a long, long life ahead of you. All of this is going to be like a bad movie you watched and you'll never watch again. I promise you that."

"I'm scared."

"Don't be. Promise me you're done with all of this for good."

"I promise."

He smiled. "That's all I ever need."

Chapter Twenty-One

Driving around town with an entire trash can full of prescription pills, which belonged to Violet Waterbury, didn't feel quite right. What if he got pulled over? What if he happened to crash his car? The what-ifs were piling up.

Where did he think he was going to take them to get rid of them? He couldn't just walk through the front door of the hotel with the trashcan full of bottles. That was a bit suspicious. He couldn't dump them where anyone could see them.

Seriously, he was at a loss and he'd promised he'd be back in an hour. That even cut out the thought that he could take them out to Eric's house, if he could even find the place.

Then Pearl popped into his head. He'd head over there and see what she had to say. At times like this he wished he had his sister's 'emergency mother kit' in the van. He could guarantee she had a big trash bag in that.

Kent parked in front of Pearl's store. He quickly climbed from the van, with the trash can, and hurried inside.

He wished he'd looked in the window first. There stood at least six people looking through racks of dresses. And by the wide eyes on two of the ladies, they'd recognized him.

Pearl moved to him and then her eyes too grew wide.

She put her arm around his shoulders and grinned. "In the back room," she commanded and hurried him away. He then heard her tell the other ladies, "Sequin find. You can never have enough sequins in old medicine bottles, right?"

The women all laughed as Kent ducked into the small room where Pearl had a table, two chairs, a small refrigerator, and a microwave.

It was ten minutes before she hurried into the room and shut the door.

Kent stood from the chair at the table. "I'm so sorry. I should have looked to see if you had customers. I didn't think to…"

"Are these her pills?"

"Her mother's pills, but yes. This is all of them."

Pearl walked over to the trash can and began pulling out the bottles and reading the labels. "This is like a freaking pharmacy. What was wrong with that stupid woman?"

"Bethany?" His voice rose in offense.

"No, her stupid mother. I never liked that woman. My dad tried to get us to, but I didn't like her. When Bethany was six, I asked him to keep her here after they had come for a visit. Stupid Violet was probably trying to scam money. She probably got it too. Poor Bethany, I remember her having marks on her."

Kent reached for Pearl's hand, stopping her from taking another bottle from the trash can. "Marks?"

"Hand marks on her arm," she said and he let go. "As if someone grabbed her arm—often."

Bethany hadn't mentioned that and he assumed it was just normal behavior for her mother to do that. Why mention it?

"She promised me this was over," he said. "I'm taking her away for the week. This is all she had and she already had it in the trash can. I think that means she's ready to move on."

"She's going to need more help than you or I can give her," Pearl pointed out.

"Maybe. But we're her first line of defense. We leave tonight and will be back next Wednesday."

"Okay. You keep in touch with me. Have her call me every day. Get her help if she needs it and…"

Kent gathered Pearl's hands in his. "I love her. I meant it when I said it. Nothing, and I mean nothing, is ever going to happen to her again."

"We have to protect her."

"We are." He kissed her on the cheek and gave her hands a gentle squeeze. "I have to get back to her. Can you make these disappear?"

"Like a Vegas magician."

"Good enough."

Kent returned within the hour he'd promised. Susan was home now. She was wiping her eyes from visible tears when she answered the door.

"Everything okay here?" he asked.

"We're having some tea and laughing so hard we're crying," she said as she walked him to the kitchen.

There sat Bethany and another woman who were both wiping away tears, just as Susan had.

Bethany stood and kissed him gently on the lips. Then she turned toward the other woman. "This is my sister Audrey."

"Nice to meet you."

"Likewise," she said, still trying to catch her breath.

"Looks like you girls are having a nice time."

Bethany rested her hand on his chest. "We are. A very nice time."

"I still have to pack. Why don't I leave you and your…"

"No," she said softly. "I'm ready to go. My bag is by the door."

"I'll go put it in the van," he said and she nodded.

He shut the front door behind him after he'd picked up her bag. He wondered what had spurred her decision to not stay and chat with the women. It should have been a good thing to stay and bond with her sister, he thought.

As he opened the side door to the van, Bethany walked out of the front door, and closed it behind her.

She was smiling. It was about time he saw that smile without having to have coaxed it out of her.

"Are you sure you don't want to stay?"

She walked toward him and wrapped her arms around his neck. He gathered her close.

"I want to be with you. You have no idea how good I feel right now."

"I'm glad."

"How long of a drive do we have?"

"Well, I have to go check out of my hotel, and then we have just shy of four hours."

She nodded with a smile. "What kind of radio does this thing have in it?"

He cringed. "AM, FM."

"iPhone hook up?"

"It's that old," he said shaking his head.

"Okay then." She nipped his lips with a gentle kiss. "How about in two hours we pull over so I can have fifteen minutes of yoga?"

He crinkled up his nose at that. "Really? You want to do yoga during the trip?"

"Would you trust me if I told you that it helps me keep my food down if I'm focused. If I tell you that I won't get restless if I stretch. If..."

"Anything you want, sweetheart. As long as you're with me the rest of the week you just tell me what you need."

"I want you to introduce me as Bethany Walker."

He eased back slightly. "Bethany Walker?"

"I've decided that if I'm going to toss away Bethany Waterbury then I should be the other me," she giggled when she said it. "Audrey came up with the idea."

"You told Audrey?"

"And Susan."

"You're recovering by leaps and bounds."

She rested her head against his chest. "Baby steps."

"Those sound good to me."

Within the hour, Kent was checked out of his hotel and they were on their way. Bethany had found some radio station with music he'd never heard before. If it wasn't country, Kent hadn't been exposed.

She was seated next to him. If she had a headband of daisies around her head, she'd have been the perfect embodiment of a 60's child of love, he thought. She was breathtaking.

"You should watch the road," she said tucking her bare feet up under her skirt.

"Sorry. Distracted by your beauty."

She laughed easily and the pink glow in her cheeks made him happy. This release for her wasn't going to be so hard, he decided.

Two hours into the drive, he found a park where they could park and she could do her yoga. The backdrop was perfect with the evening sun.

Though she had tried her best to convince him to do yoga with her, he insisted that he'd much rather watch her. It proved to be the better choice. Watching her beautiful body bend and move in a fluid dance was breathtaking.

The drive took more than four hours with their stop half-way and then a necessary dinner break.

Kent watched as Bethany searched the menu for a meal. Even though she settled on a salad, he thought that was a step in the right direction. There was no gorging yourself on a salad. Not that he could imagine anyway.

When they finally checked into their hotel, it was nearly nine o'clock. It was then he noticed Bethany's fidgeting.

"Everything okay?"

"Yep. I feel good. Just have a lot of energy."

He gave her a small nod. "What do you want to do with that?"

It didn't take but a moment and she was jumping into his arms, her legs wrapped around his waist, and his balance compromised, dumping them both onto the bed.

"This is a fine idea," he said as she took him under with a kiss as he unbuttoned his shirt.

At some point, he'd have to seriously consider if this was the best method to keep her clean and sober, but for now it seemed like a perfectly legitimate way.

Chapter Twenty-Two

Kent had three signings in South Carolina in two days. They would be very busy and he had given it a lot of thought. Bethany was used to being busy. Downtime for the past few months wasn't her style.

She'd talked about some of the brighter sides of her career and living in Hollywood during their four-hour drive. He wasn't sure she even realized she was opening up to him as much as she was.

She'd worked on movie sets, even if she wasn't in the cast. It seemed she had a good eye for detail and the set designers let her help out on more than one occasion.

She was the face of Esquire Denim Company too. He hadn't known that, but then he'd quickly realized he'd never heard of the company.

On a laugh, she'd told him it had gone under before it had started, but it was a good experience.

There had been a lot of table waiting at restaurants. Retail was not her favorite job choice and she didn't enjoy pizza delivery either.

No matter what job it was, though, Bethany had always seemed to have more than one at a time.

"I'm going to introduce you as my assistant," Kent said as he checked his tie in the mirror outside the first bookstore.

"That makes you sound important."

He chuckled. "Yeah, it does, doesn't it?"

"Okay, Mr. Black. What does your assistant have to do?"

He pushed his hair around with his fingers and closed the mirror. "Just do what you did at the book signing at the Garden Room."

Her smile faded. "So I'll be right there with you?"

"Yes, and your name is Bethany Walker, so no one will recognize you."

"Just because that's my name doesn't mean…"

"Trust me. The minute you tell them you're not *her* that will be that."

She took in a deep breath. "Okay then. Miss Walker is here to serve you."

He felt the heat move into his cheeks and she must have noticed because she rested her hand on his thigh and gave it a squeeze. "Later, Mr. Black."

Kent hadn't quite realized the scope of Bethany's acting ability. While he'd been talking to the store manager, Bethany had dismissed herself to look around.

She'd worn another long skirt today, not quite as bohemian as the one she'd worn on their drive, but flowy. As the manager got Kent set up at his table, she'd managed to sneak away to the bathroom, pin up her hair, and now she had glasses?

"Where did you get those?" he asked when she returned from the restroom.

"Little boutique next door had them. They're fake, but cute, don't you think?" She adjusted them with her fingers.

"You look studious."

"I look like an assistant."

He laughed and gave her hand a squeeze as the first people walked through the door and the line began to form. It was time, for just a few hours, to not think about Bethany, but to think about himself. This was what made his life so easy and so free. He had to focus now on his readers.

Bethany handed him books, open to the specific page he preferred to sign on. She'd run to Starbucks and brought him back a drink. She'd even talked to his sister when she'd called and told him he'd call her back. It would be interesting to see what each of them thought of the other after a few brief moments on the phone.

He was an hour into his signing before someone walked up to the side of the table and tapped Bethany on the shoulder. "You're Bethany Waterbury."

Kent was quick to turn in his seat, but Bethany placed her hands folded in her lap and smiled at the man. "That is a huge compliment, but no. I'm not her."

"You have to be."

"Again, thank you. She's beautiful. I'm Beth Walker," she said shortening her name and holding her hand out to shake the man's hand.

He studied her and shook her hand. "I'm sorry, ma'am. I could have sworn you were her."

"I get that a lot, actually."

He nodded and walked away.

"Beth?" Kent whispered.

"My mother would never let me shorten it. She's not here is she?" she asked. She picked up another book with a smile and handed it to him for the next person who came to the table.

Bethany felt free with her plastic glasses and her new name. This was the most uplifting moment of her life. How was that possible? Beth Walker, assistant to Mr. Kent Black. Oh, God, it was as if she'd died and gone to heaven.

When the manager of the store came by the table in his second hour, he knelt down next to her and asked if they'd like sandwiches from the deli down the mall. She very professionally gave him their orders and even that was uplifting.

In the course of the day, a few more people had asked her about being Bethany Waterbury. She had a calm ease about her telling them that wasn't her.

By the time Kent's signing was over, her fear of being seen with him was gone. No one could touch her as long as this man was with her.

When they reached his van, she pulled him to her and kissed him as hard as she could.

"What was that for?"

"For giving me my life back."

He narrowed his gaze on her. "One day of giving out a fake name behind fake glasses isn't going to solve anything."

"No, but my heart is so full right now. Your sister said I sounded beautiful too, by the way."

"She'd be right about that."

"Anyway," she said pulling her hair from the knot on her head. "I'm ready to be Beth Walker. Susan said I could design floral arrangements for her. I could be your assistant. I don't have to be that person I was before."

"Is that what you want? You want to give it all away?"

"It's not worth fighting for, Kent. Bethany Waterbury was more fake than Beth Walker could ever be."

"I'm not sure of that name change," he said nipping her nose with a kiss. "We may have to talk about that."

He walked around the side of the van before she could ask him about that. Before he got into the van, his phone rang and he answered it as he started the engine.

"I promise to read you a story tonight," he said as he backed out of the parking space. "You want a story about a dinosaur? Okay, I'll find you a dinosaur story." He nodded as he listened. "Two more weeks. Yes, then I'll push you on the rope swing."

Kent finished his call and set the phone in the cup holder. Bethany said, "I don't want to ask, but who was that?"

"My nephew. I read to him almost every night. Tonight he wants dinosaurs."

"That's precious."

"You have to read to kids early to get them into reading. Studies show that it helps."

"Yes, and he has parents, but you take the time to be in his life even when you're not there with him."

He shrugged as if it were no big deal. "He's important to me. They all are."

Bethany sunk into her seat and gazed out the window. She couldn't help but wonder what that would be like—to have been that important.

Kent decided that the best place to get a dinosaur book would be at the store he had a signing at in the morning. The owners always liked when you were a patron too.

Bethany walked, hand in hand, with him down the aisles. "Do you read to your nieces too?"

"When they sit still long enough."

"Maybe you should get them a book."

He smiled and gave her hand a squeeze. "Pick one."

"Oh, this *Frozen* one is a must. If they are little girls, they have to love Anna and Elsa."

"That's the one with the snowman, right?"

She laughed. "Yes. It's very cute."

"You watch Disney movies?"

She rested her head on his shoulder. "Every chance I can get."

He'd have to remember that.

They met with the owner, purchased a dinosaur book and a Disney Princess book, and headed back to the hotel room where his computer chimed before he could even get settled.

When he logged in, his sister's face appeared on the screen.

"I have a little boy who can't wait for his story," she said.

"I bought a new book. Bethany bought one for the girls too," he said yanking her in front of the computer screen. "Cassie, this is Bethany."

His sister smiled. "Hello."

"Hi," Bethany's voice cracked. "It's nice to meet you. I've heard a lot about you."

"Likewise."

A little head moved into the view of the camera and a moment later his nephew was on his mother's lap.

"Who's that?" He pointed at the screen and right in Bethany's direction.

"This is Bethany."

She waved as his nephew wrinkled up his nose. "Is she your girlfriend?"

"How do you know about girlfriends?" he asked and then nodded. "Yes, she's my girlfriend."

He studied her through the computer. "I want her to read my dinosaurs."

Kent looked at Bethany's face. Her eyes were wide and she appeared to be scared to death. It humored him.

"You heard the boy," he said. "Bethany, this is Cole." He pointed to the screen.

"Hello," she said softly. "Are you sure you want me to read this to you instead of your uncle?"

"Yup."

"She got a book for your sister too," he said as another little head appeared in the shot and his sister lifted his niece up on her lap. "Hey, my girl. Sara, this is Bethany."

She waved sweetly.

"She bought you a *Frozen* story for tonight."

That was met with a squeal, but then Cole began to demand his story.

Bethany sat down and he turned the computer so it was on her. It was then the magic started as she read the books and the stories came to life. The kids laughed and cheered for the mighty dinosaur named Clive. She read it twice before she began to read adventures of Anna and Elsa, at which time Cole disappeared, but Sara sat and intently listened.

When the stories were over he blew them all kisses, and so did Bethany. Then she excused herself to the bathroom to get ready for bed.

"She seems nice," Cassie said.

"She is."

"You're bringing her here?"

"When I come for my signing."

She nodded. "Be careful, Kent."

He didn't like her tone and he certainly didn't need Bethany picking up on it. "I am. I love you. Talk to you tomorrow," he said as he closed the computer.

Once his sister got something stuck in her head, it was hard to get it out. She was afraid for him. That was understandable. But he loved Bethany. Nothing was going to happen to break him—or her. He was absolutely sure of it. His sister was going to have to deal with that.

Chapter Twenty- Three

Kent had to admit, watching the transformation of Bethany into Beth over the week was entertaining. Each stop they made, Beth had something added to her. First it was the glasses. The next day it was the decorative sticks that went into the pile of hair on her head. She had a certain fashion too and by the last stop, she had on a black suit.

Okay, the sexy assistant was someone he absolutely could enjoy.

It never failed, though, someone approached her at every stop, and even at hotels, wanting the autograph of Bethany Waterbury. But *Beth* insisted they were misled.

He was proud of her transformation of herself too. Through their stays in South Carolina, into Tennessee, and their final stop in Alabama, Beth was opening up and taking back some of the control she'd lost. Kent wasn't a fool to think that in one week, twenty-four years of abuse from her mother, an industry, and herself could be corrected. But he could see the progress and he hoped she saw it and felt it too.

"Susan just texted me," she said one night as she rested in his arms on the hotel bed. The TV played an old movie in black and white. It was Jimmy Stewart and that imaginary bunny, which she had to remind him his name was Harvey.

"What did she want?"

"She has a bridal shower to cater next week. She wants me to help serve and do the centerpieces."

"That's nice." He kissed the top of her head.

"Glenda is going to help too."

"Her future mother-in-law, right?"

She nodded and turned to look at him. "Where do you have to head off to after that?"

He cupped her face in his hand. "Texas. I have four dates there and an extended promised stay at my parents' house."

She sank in next to him again. "How extended?"

"I don't know. How long do you want to stay?"

Now she sat up and turned toward him fully. "You want me to go home with you?"

"Yes."

"I've never been really good with parents. I mean look at mine."

"Yeah, mine are different."

"I'm not sure your sister likes me much."

He posed a hurtful face. "I think she likes you just fine. She's let you read that Frozen book to her daughters ever night this week."

Bethany rolled her eyes and let out a small snort. "She tolerated it."

"She's worried about me."

"Because of who I am?"

"Because I love you and haven't known you that long," he said as convincingly as he could. "I'm not a guy who dates or gets out of my hotel room except to go to book signings. She thinks it's a bit odd I find some attractive woman and fall in love."

"You really love me?"

He reached for her and pulled her to him. "I do."

Bethany rested against him, her head against his heart. "Are you staying in Georgia until you leave again?"

"I am. And I'll be looking for a place to live. I think that's where I'm going to settle down now. It's time."

She gazed up at him. "Stay with me for now. Susan is going to move out soon. I'll need a roommate."

"You want me to live with you?"

She rose to kiss him gently on the lips. "Forever."

Yes, that's what he wanted too. It was much too early to discuss it, but he was sure that's what he wanted.

Huntsville, Alabama was his last stop on this specific tour. Kent hadn't been getting much writing done with Bethany around and he didn't realize just how much of a workaholic he was. All these years living in hotel rooms, he'd netted a lot of hours and a lot of books.

He had deadlines looming now and a meeting with a producer over the new book they wanted to make into a movie. With a lot of thought, he didn't want Bethany around for that. How strange their lives should cross in such a manner.

As *Beth* readied herself for the day, Kent watched her. Was this how she got ready for a part? Did she build the character a day at a time, adding tweaks until they were perfect? Sure, *Beth* was her. It wasn't really a character as much as a disguise to remain normal. He chuckled to himself. Now that sounded silly, but at the same time made a whole lot of sense.

Bethany smacked her lips together after applying lipstick and looked herself over.

"You're perfect," he said from his stance leaning against the wall.

"It'll do." She placed her hands on her stomach and he lurched toward her.

"Are you okay? Are you not feeling well?"

She laughed and turned. "You're jumpy and my stomach is growling. I'm starving."

He shook his head in embarrassment. "You're starving? That's a good thing, right?"

"Everything, and I mean everything, I've eaten this week has stayed down. I promise you. And look, I'll prove it." She lifted up her blouse to reveal the taunt tug on the button of her skirt. "It's not much, but for the first time in my life my clothes are a little tight."

It was worth scooping her up and messing up that lipstick. "I love it. Let's go eat."

Pancakes had always been a favorite for Bethany. Evil for Violet Waterbury, but Bethany didn't care anymore.

"Is it hard to write a book?" she asked, covering her mouth with her hand since her mouth was full.

"For me, no. For others, yes."

"For me?"

He lowered his fork and studied her. "You want to write a book?"

She shrugged. "I don't know. I always was fascinated by script writing. It's not too much different, is it?"

"Night and day, but the creative part is more or less the same. What do you want to write about?"

"I don't know. A billionaire who falls in love with a normal, everyday girl."

She saw him stifle his laugh and she appreciated it.

Wiping his mouth with his napkin, he then lowered it to his lap. "You have to start writing. The best advice I can give you is to just get it out. It doesn't have to be good, it just has to be."

"I should look into getting a laptop."

"You can use mine for now. We'll be at the bookstore for four hours. It has a nice, cozy coffee shop. You could go write."

"But, *Beth* is there to help you."

"*Beth*, can go write her blockbuster."

She laughed. "A book by Beth Walker."

"I like it," he said toasting her with his coffee.

"I do too."

And so she began. With Kent's laptop on the small coffee table in front of her, Bethany began to write the story brewing in her head. Every line she read was very elementary and she didn't like it at all. But it wasn't about what it looked like now, he had told her. Just get the story down.

She'd been sitting there writing for nearly two hours when the chair across from her moved and someone sat down.

Quickly she finished her sentence before she looked up and her heart slammed into her chest.

"Bethany Waterbury. I thought that was you."

She swallowed hard and looked next to her where she'd set the fake glasses. Quickly she slid them on.

"I'm sorry. My name is Beth Walker. I'm not..."

"That's cute. Took your daddy's last name?" He leaned back in his chair and crossed his legs.

The black custom suit and blue tie was his style. The expensive sunglasses that still shaded his eyes didn't take the heat out of them.

"Like I said, I'm not who you think..."

He leaned in, placed his hand on the computer screen, and closed it. "Don't mess with me. As someone who has seen you naked and stoned, I think I know who the hell you are."

Her teeth chattered and every muscle in her body clenched. She refused to cry. She refused to draw attention to herself at all. But suddenly those pancakes weren't settled and she knew she couldn't just get up from the table.

"Why are you here?" she finally gathered enough courage to ask.

"Why are you? I heard your pathetic mother died and you ran out of town. Had a contract you breached too. Nice way to leave an impression." He reached for her hand and she pulled away.

"I don't belong in Hollywood anymore."

"You never really did. You and your mother just knew how to work deals, if you know what I mean." He ran his tongue over his teeth. "I'm not here for you anyway. Wouldn't waste my time. See that guy over there?" He nodded toward Kent. "That's where the talent is. That's the kind of man I'm out to work for. You should go introduce yourself," he said as he stood. "Maybe he could beg to have you in his movies and then you could get on your knees for him," he laughed as he walked away.

Bethany was violently sick now.

She gathered the laptop and ran to the back of the store where there was a bathroom. She locked the door and vomited hard, so hard that tears rolled down her cheeks and soon there was blood.

Her head spun and she sat down against the wall and sobbed.

She had to get out of there—out of Alabama and away from Kent Black.

Chapter Twenty-Four

Kent looked toward the coffee shop where Bethany had been sitting, but he didn't see her. He'd have gone to look for her, but the line of readers was out the door. Now was the time he could use *Beth*.

As he looked around, between greeting people with a smile that was now straining his cheeks, he saw Dez Armstrong headed toward him. What the hell? The producer that wanted to talk movie deals was in Huntsville, Alabama?

"Hey, Kent, how are you?" He was coming at him with his hand extended and ready to shake.

Kent stood and greeted him. "Hi. How are you? What are you doing here?" He rambled even with Hollywood people when he was nervous.

"Wanted to hunt you down. Talk to you about *Quantum*. It's doing great on the charts. The studio thinks it could be a big deal in the theaters. The last was killer and it's good to be a franchise," he said with a laugh that sounded near sinister as he rested his hand on Kent's shoulder.

"Great. Maybe I can call you and we could meet."

"I'm here now. The bookstore said you're done in a half hour."

"I don't know. We're pretty lucky to still have a line," he said.

Dez shrugged. "They'll buy it anyway. You're a big deal. You have to act like a big deal."

"Right, well…"

Dez took his card from his jacket pocket. "As soon as you're done. You call me. Let's get this thing tied up."

Kent nodded as he took the card and continued to scan the store for Bethany.

Dez turned to walk away as a very excited woman approached the table. She'd already grabbed Kent's hands and was shaking both of them, professing her extreme love for his work when Dez turned back and lifted his dark glasses.

"Hey, Black," he called out. "Bethany Waterbury, you heard of her?"

Kent's mouth went dry and he stared at the man as the woman continued to talk to him.

"She's lurking around here. Maybe she wants a role in your movie. Couldn't hurt her career which is tanked." He laughed with a wave and walked out of the store.

The woman holding his hands continued to talk to him. He managed to get a book and sign it for her, somehow sending her on her way, as he signaled the owner of the store.

"My assistant. Have you seen her?"

The woman nodded and pulled a note from her pocket. "She left just a bit ago. She handed this to one of my clerks and walked out with a laptop under her arm."

He opened the note. HAD TO LEAVE. TOOK CAB BACK.

If she was trying to be cryptic about something that was wrong, she wasn't doing a very good job. He was now panicked and his mind scattered to the million things that could go wrong.

He looked at the line beyond his table. There were about twenty more people and it looked as though they had roped off the entrance. Okay, he could do this, he thought. He'd finish the signing. Buy a few new books he could pull off the shelves for his nieces and nephews, then head back. Hopefully, Bethany was okay.

Within thirty minutes, he was in the van and headed toward the hotel. A bag of books he didn't really even look at from the children's section, in the seat next to him.

He'd called Bethany four times, but she hadn't answered her phone. The closer to the hotel he got, the more worried he became.

Kent parked the van in two spaces. The worst parking job he'd ever done, but it just didn't matter right now. He had to get to her.

He hurried through the hotel and to the room. Slipping his key card into the door, he pushed it open. The room was still and dark. The housekeeper had made the bed and usually opened the drapes. That said to him that Bethany had been there.

He opened the closet and only his clothes remained.

On the table was his laptop.

He opened it quickly and saw that whatever she'd written that day was still on the screen. The last sentence wasn't even finished.

Quickly he called down to the front desk and asked if they'd seen her.

"She asked for a rental car. We had to send her in a taxi to get one."

Kent hung up the phone, sat down on the bed, and buried his head in his hands.

She'd left him.

She'd just left him.

~*~

The damn attendant at the car rental had even asked for an autograph. Bethany swore that she'd never, ever give out another autograph as long as she lived. Bethany Waterbury was as dead to her now as Violet Waterbury.

Tears rolled from her eyes as she drove down the now dark highway. She had to get back to Georgia, collect her car, and leave. She didn't know where. She just had to leave.

She'd turned off her cell phone so that no one could find her. The map the car rental place had given her had fallen between the seats. All she could hope for was that she was headed in the right direction.

Since the minute Dez had sat down across from her, her heart hammered in her chest. She felt vile and dirty.

With a good amount of power, she whacked the heel of her hand against the steering wheel and screamed.

That man had manipulated her and used her since she was fifteen. He'd sexually used her as a pawn in his games. She'd awakened in his bed more than once and not known how she got there. How many rounds of pills had he purchased for her mother so that she'd pass out and he could be Bethany's savior? "Just come home with me. She'll be okay," he'd say.

Kent didn't deserve to have a woman like her in his life. Her family didn't deserve to have a bad seed like her. Pearl was too kind and Audrey too innocent. Todd kept to himself and didn't look for trouble and Jake lived life fast, he'd never notice she wasn't in Georgia.

Even her own father would probably forget she'd been there in a week.

Susan…oh, Susan crossed her mind. She was more of a sister than her own sisters. She might be devastated to find Bethany gone and moved away. But there had to be somewhere she didn't accidently fall into a crowd that once knew her.

It wasn't Kent's fault that their worlds somehow collided. He deserved his successes. He worked hard. Those books were his life—at least they were until she'd shown up.

Bethany reached for her purse and shook it out in the seat next to her. There was always a bottle of something in there to keep her calm.

But now there wasn't. She'd thrown it all away, just as she'd promised Kent she would. No, she'd have to cry her way all the way back to Georgia, because she had nothing to suppress the pain she was feeling.

Once she was back, she could pack up and move on. She'd get help. Yes, that's what she'd do. She'd get some help.

She'd drive to Atlanta and check into a rehab center. She'd legally change her name and she'd go on with her life—alone.

Chapter Twenty-Five

It was nearly midnight when Bethany walked through the front door of the silent house. Both Susan and Eric were gone.

Immediately it came to mind that perhaps their house was complete. Her father had said it was nearly done. Maybe they'd gone to stay there.

All the better, she thought. She didn't need anyone to ask her questions.

Walking into the house, she went straight for the kitchen. She pulled down a mug and filled it with water. There wasn't time in her mind to wait to boil water for tea any other way than to put it in the microwave.

She watched it as it went around and around in circles and thought it mimicked her life so much. Short bursts of energy running around and around until everything exploded.

All of it hurt so bad, she could hardly breathe.

Inside of her, she felt as though she were screaming in the silent house. Was this bravery? Bravery to admit she needed help? Sure, but cowardly to want to leave and find help. Above all else she simply didn't want to hurt anyone else in her life. And, she didn't want to be hurt anymore.

When the microwave buzzed in completion, she carefully pulled the mug out and inserted a tea bag from the canister on the counter. By now Kent had to know she was gone. If she turned on her phone, she'd probably find a dozen calls from him.

If he tried to follow her home, she'd be gone before he got there. Right now she was going to head up to her room. Draw a warm bath, drink her tea, and pack her belongings. She'd leave very early tomorrow morning and head to

Atlanta. She'd get a hotel room, research rehab facilities, and get her life in order.

She closed her bedroom door and went to the bathroom to start the bathtub. Undressing, she kicked her clothes toward the door. She'd pack them last.

She opened the now nearly empty cabinet behind the mirror. Her toothbrush, toothpaste, deodorant, razor, and the bath salts remained.

Taking the salts, she sprinkled them into the tub. The scent of lavender filled the air and the tension in her body began to ease.

A few candles would be nice too, she thought. As she turned around, she dropped the container of salts into the tub, splashing water all over the floor.

Her mood must have lightened slightly, because she actually laughed. She mopped up most of the water that had splashed out onto the floor with the floor mat, put on her robe, and went out into her bedroom to find the candles she had in the drawer.

She'd kept them in the drawer of the nightstand, next to her bed. She'd bought them in a cute boutique in town owned by a young Italian woman, whom she'd found very charming.

Bethany pulled open the drawer, saw the candles, and the last remaining bottle of her mother's pills.

Clenching her hands tightly, she stared down into the drawer. It was if they were sharp or poisonous. She didn't want to put her hand inside and pull them out, but she had to. They had to be disposed of—destroyed.

Taking a deep breath, Bethany reached in and pulled the bottle out of the drawer.

They were sleeping pills. She should have remembered they were there, but it had slipped her mind.

Bethany hurried to the bathroom. They had to be flushed. They had to be sent away where she'd never, ever see them again.

As she walked through the door, she twisted the top off the bottle. The water was near to the top of the tub and she reached over to turn it off. The floor was still wet and the floor mat bunched under her feet, sending Bethany and the bottle of pills backward. Her back hit the side of the toilet and then her head hit. Pills flew all around her as her head bounced on the floor.

Bethany looked up at the lights which seemed very bright now, meekly she tried to yell for help though no one was around. The lights seemed to fan out and then grew darker and darker.

~*~

Kent sat on the edge of his bed, his phone in his hand. He hated that he'd sent Susan into hysterics when he'd told her that Bethany had rented a car and left without a word. Explaining what had happened and adding the information he'd found about Dez Armstrong online, he was sick to his stomach wondering what the man had done to her once to cause her to have this kind of reaction.

Susan had promised she'd call the moment she had word on Bethany. They'd been out at the new house. It would take them nearly an hour to get home, but she'd call.

So now he waited.

His sister Skyped and thankfully hadn't given him any crap about Bethany and what kind of woman she was. Instead she said, "I hope she's okay. Mom is looking forward to meeting her."

"She hasn't done her homework online yet? The Internet hasn't ruined Bethany for her?"

"You're not being nice. Yes, she's found out a lot about her and she feels sorry for her. She's not as shallow as you make her out to be."

He pinched the bridge of his nose. "I just don't want people making opinions about her based on what the tabloids or the Internet has said. She's not that person…really." He wished he hadn't added that, but his sister was bound to find out about the *true* Bethany if he ever found her and got her to agree to stay with him.

He'd ended the call with his sister, ordered room service, and paced. If he didn't hear from Susan soon, he was going to jump in the car and…

His phone rang.

"Hello," his voice broke as he answered.

"It's Susan," she said, but her voice cracked. Was she crying?

"Do you have her? Did she make it home?" He was on his feet.

"Um, yeah. She was home," he heard her voice shake again. Something was wrong. This wasn't a calm *oh, yeah she's home* phone call.

"Susan, what's going on?"

Now he could hear the crying. "We got home. She was there. She was in the bathroom. The tub was full."

Kent gripped his chest as his heart was already breaking and the pain was excruciating. Did she have to finish the sentence?

Susan cleared her throat. "She was on the floor. There was blood. She hit her head. And pills. Pills were everywhere."

Kent's throat closed off and he was barely able to muster the words, "Is she dead?"

Her mother's tragedy played in his head vividly as if he were there the day Bethany had found her.

"No. No," she said again with more vigor. "She's in the hospital. They won't let me see her. They let her father in, but he's the only one."

Kent went straight for the closet, pulled out his suitcase, and began shoving things into it as Susan gasped for breath.

"I didn't know it was this bad," she said.

"I have a feeling that someone from her past might have run into her today and sent her over the edge." He cursed under his breath. "I thought she gave me all the pills."

"I don't know. They were sleeping pills and they were her mother's," Susan confirmed. "She must have dropped them because they were all over."

"I'm headed out. I'll be there in less than five hours."

~*~

Bethany winced at the lights when the doctor shined them in her eyes.

"Pupils are looking better. She needs to stay under watch, though. That was a nasty fall."

Someone squeezed her hand and when she turned she saw her father there. "How are you feeling?"

She tried to talk but found her throat was raw. "Horrible."

"Bethany," the other man directed her attention to him. "We've done some blood work and as a precautionary measure, since you were unconscious, we pumped your stomach. You had no sign of drugs in your system, but there were sleeping pills found next to you. Did you take those pills, Bethany?"

Her father squeezed her hand again.

"No," her voice was weak. "No. I flushed them."

Her father leaned in. "No, honey. The bottle was in your hand and there were pills everywhere. You were in your robe and the tub was full."

She tried to move, but her head throbbed. She lifted her hand to feel it, but it was full of wires and lines of fluid poked into her skin.

She focused on her father. "I went home to relax. I left Kent in Alabama." She winced. Kent. It was a horrible way to end things, just to leave him as she had. "I came home to pack. I wanted to drive to Atlanta and check into a rehab center."

"Rehab? Why?"

Bethany turned away. "I didn't want to turn into my mother," she said softly.

"Oh, honey. You're nothing like your mother."

"I need help, Dad." She turned back to him. "Or I'll die too."

The doctor looked at the monitors. "You didn't take any of the pills then?"

"No." She swallowed to moisten her throat. "I found the last bottle in a drawer. I was going to flush them. I must have slipped and fallen."

"You hit your head. We got it stitched up. X-rays didn't show internal bleeding. Perhaps this afternoon, if your numbers stay up, we can send you home."

"No," she said, wishing she had the energy to sit up. "I can't go home. I need help. Please help me."

The doctor smiled. "I'll have a counselor come in and discuss rehab options with you."

"Thank you," she said as she eased against the bed.

As soon as the doctor left the room her father leaned in and kissed her cheek. He'd never done that before, she realized.

"I'm proud of you. It takes a very strong woman to ask for help like that."

"I'm not strong. I'm weak. That's why I took them. That's why I don't eat. I need my life back." She took a breath. "I want to change my name to Walker," she said. "I don't want to be who I was."

Now her father was smiling. "Okay, we'll talk about all of that when you're all better."

~*~

Kent rushed into the hospital and stopped immediately. The entire lobby was full of people and some of them he knew. The others he assumed were the rest of Bethany's family.

Susan saw him first and ran to him, wrapping her arms around him and sobbing on his shoulder.

"She's okay. She's going to be okay."

He eased her back, holding onto her arms. "How many pills did she take?"

A man walked up next to them. "She didn't take any. She was trying to flush them away when she fell."

Susan stepped back as the man held his hand out to Kent. "Byron Walker," he introduced himself.

"Kent Black, sir. I'm a friend of Bethany's. Well, I'm more than a friend, sir. We've been seeing each other. Though I don't know if we still are. She left me in Alabama, but I love your daughter. I really do. And…"

Byron Walker laughed and placed his hand on Kent's shoulder. "She said when you're nervous you ramble."

"Yes, sir. I do." He swallowed hard. "She told you about me?"

The man smiled. "She did. She's not going to see you now."

"Oh. Well, I understand."

"Let's take a walk."

Kent nodded and followed Byron out the front door of the hospital. Byron stood on the front step and tucked his hands into his front pockets.

"Everything about this is like her mother," he said.

"I'm not sure she'd like to hear you say that," Kent added, hoping he hadn't overstepped his boundary.

"She wouldn't. But the things I see in her are the good things about her mother. Not the bad things she saw."

"Oh. With all due respect, I haven't heard a lot of good things about her mother."

"I wouldn't suppose you would." He turned to him and looked him square in the eye. "You love her."

"More than anything. I'm just not sure she feels the same way."

Her father nodded and then clucked his tongue. "I wouldn't say that. I think she's confused and afraid she'll hurt you."

"It hurts knowing she wouldn't be around me for that reason."

Bryon gave him a nod and then began to walk. Kent quickly followed. They were silent until they rounded the side of the building.

"She asked me to put her in rehab. She said that had been her plan."

"That's a brave thing. To ask for help."

Her father smiled, his head still lowered and his eyes to the ground as they walked. "That's what I told her."

"Can I visit her? I want her to know I support her. In fact, on my drive here, I called that producer, the one I think set her off, and told him he could kiss my ass. I'd never let one of my books be produced into Hollywood crap by him."

Bryon stopped. "You turned down a movie deal for her?"

"I don't know anything about their relationship. Maybe she didn't even know him, but something told me it was a bad deal. I couldn't let her be around that."

Byron turned to him. "She didn't say much about him, but I think a lot of her pain stems from him and others like him."

"Then my books remain books. There's no need for people to see movies made by people who hurt people."

Her father studied him. "I like you."

"Oh, good." He let out a breath he'd held and didn't know it. "I just want her to."

Byron began to walk again and Kent kept his slowed pace.

"She'll be in the rehab center for a month and has asked that no one knows where she is and no one visits."

"Okay, though that's going to kill me."

"I think too much of her mother is still following her and she doesn't need it leaked anywhere."

"I understand."

Byron ran his hand over the back of his neck. "She wants to change her name to Walker too. She should have been a Walker from the day she was born," he said with a hint of regret vibrating in his voice.

"She is a Walker. I see the dynamic the family has. She fits in."

"Yes, she does."

This time Kent stopped and after a few steps Bryan turned and stopped. "Sir, I think Walker is a fine name. She'd wear it well, but when she's out, I'd like to ask her to consider changing her name to Black."

Byron walked toward him and stood nearly toe to toe with him. Though he was shorter, Kent was horribly intimated by him.

"You want to marry her?"

"Yes, sir. That's been my intent all along."

"What if she says no?"

"Then she should be a Walker. I won't leave though until she asks me to."

The smile resurfaced. "In one month, when she's out, you let me know what she decides. Either way, I think I'd like to see that name changed."

From the first time since *Beth* had sat down in the corner of the coffee shop yesterday and began to pen her story, Kent smiled. Perhaps this saga wasn't over just yet.

Epilogue

Bethany looked at herself in the mirror of the room in which she'd spent the past month. She was ten pounds healthier and it showed in the bright yellow, flowered dress she wore. For the first time, she didn't judge herself on that merit. She just looked beautiful, she thought.

Her hair was brighter too and she gave it a toss over her shoulder. She was glad that Susan had given the dress to her father to bring to her to wear home.

Over the course of the month, she'd done a lot of growing and a lot of forgiving. Violet Waterbury would have greatly benefitted from such an opportunity. Bethany was grateful she'd been able to take control of her own life. Who's to say things would have gotten better even though she'd decided on rehab? Maybe if she'd taken that bath and headed out of town, she'd never have looked back. Maybe she'd to be dead now.

That wasn't the kind of thinking she was programmed with now though. No, this Bethany had a new outlook on things. She was a positive and successful woman, who would always attend meetings to remind herself just how far she'd come.

Though through it all she couldn't help but think of Kent and wonder what he'd ever done after she'd left him. Surely Dez Armstrong had signed his movie deal and things would be moving in a wonderful direction for Kent. He deserved success. He was extremely talented.

A nurse tapped on her door and she saw her in the mirror.

"I like that dress, Ms. Waterbury."

"Ms. Walker, please."

"Right." The nurse walked in and stood by the bed where her suitcase sat. "Are you ready to go?"

Bethany took in a deep breath and gave herself, and the nurse, a nod in the mirror.

"I actually think I am."

The walk down the hallway was a long one. On the other side of those doors was the world she'd been locked away from for a month. It had been her choice, but the controlled atmosphere inside was easier to navigate.

"The doctor is going to sign your release forms and send you on your way," she said opening the door to a conference room. "Just wait in here for a few moments."

Bethany walked into the room and set her suitcase on the floor. As the nurse said, the doctor came in a few minutes later, signed the papers, and gave her final instructions.

"Above all else, you call us if you need anything. Even if it's just a reassuring voice to get you through a meal."

Bethany nodded.

"I think your ride is here. Let me go get them."

Bethany tucked the papers into her purse and stood to gather her suitcase. Her father had been her only contact and he'd promised to pick her up on this, her release day.

When the door opened, she looked up and felt her mouth absolutely fall open.

Standing before her was Kent, suit coat, loose tie, and hair much too long. In his hands, he carried a huge bouquet of daisies and a gift bag dangled from his wrist.

"My sister said these would be a welcome flower. As in welcome out, welcome home, welcome…" He stopped and dropped his shoulders. "Bethany, you look amazing."

"Why are you here? Where is my father?"

"He's just outside. I can get him. I didn't know if you'd want to see me or not, so…"

She didn't let him finish his thought. She dove at him and kissed him so hard on the mouth they both fell over and into the wall. With a laugh, she pulled back, the daisy petals falling to the ground.

"Sorry."

"Oh, God, don't be. I guess you're okay that I'm here?"

"I left you. I didn't expect to see you ever again."

"Yeah, that wasn't going to work." He looked around the room. "Do you think they'd let us sit for a moment?"

Bethany nodded and took the first seat to her left and he took the one next to her.

Kent set the now abused bouquet of daisies on the table and gathered the gift bag in his hands.

"I took some liberties this month with some of your work."

"My work?"

"Yeah," he let out a sigh. "You had written a story on my computer."

She felt the heat rise in her cheeks. "Oh, you didn't read that, did you? I really was just messing around."

"I did read it. Then I read it to my sister and to my nieces."

She winced. "They hate me. Don't they?"

"No. They loved it. I realize you hadn't quite finished it and I wouldn't have imagined that what you were writing was a children's book."

"Fairy tales always have happily ever afters. I like those best, anyway."

"That's what we thought. So Sara helped make an ending to your story."

"Your niece?"

"Yes. Two-year-olds are very prolific." He pulled from the bag a children's book and handed it to her. "I had my cover designer illustrate it. With today's publishing options,

I had a few made. I think it could be a bestseller. You could do book signings with me. We'd have two lines at each store."

Bethany batted away the tears in her eyes. "You did this for me?"

"I did it for me too. I missed you too much. I had to keep busy. Had to keep you near me."

She opened the book and looked at the drawings and her words. "I've never had a gift that meant so much."

"I'll change the cover too."

"Why?"

"I took some liberties there."

She realized she hadn't looked at the cover enough, so she turned the book over and there it said *written by Bethany Black*

She lifted her tear-filled eyes to him. "What does this mean?"

"I know you wanted to change your name. I think that one fits you. I'd like you to have it."

"You want me to have your name?"

He nodded. "I want you to have it because I want you to be my wife."

She couldn't even see now through the tears and she was sure the little bit of mascara she'd put on was now streaked down her cheeks. But what the hell did it matter now.

Kent scooted his chair closer to her. "Your dad said he'd like Walker or Black. It didn't matter to him. It only mattered what you thought."

"Oh, Kent. I don't know that you really want to…"

"I want to show you something else," he cut off her thought.

She nodded and he pulled a piece of paper out of his jacket pocket and opened it for her to see.

Redhead, glorious redhead in a yellow flowered sundress, was written in pen in his handwriting.

"What is this?"

"The day I saw you at the coffee shop with your brother, I wrote this note. I wanted to remember you and thought I'd never see you again."

"You wanted to remember me?"

"I still believe in fate. Fate put me in that shop for a reason. And Lydia having me as a guest at her book club, that was fate too."

Bethany reached for his hands and gathered them in hers. "I never believed in fate before. I think I'm beginning to."

"Susan let me stay in her house when they moved. If you'd like me to move out, I…"

"Don't you dare. I want you there with me," she said inching in closer to him. "And I like the name on the book, just the way it is."

"Bethany Black?"

"For the rest of my life."

We hope you enjoyed the second installment of
THE WALKERS

Here is a sneak peek into the third book in the series
WALKER BRIDE

Please visit us at www.5princebooks.com for updated
release information on this and other books in the series.

Chapter One ~ Walker Bride

Ivory satin smoothed under her fingers. Each pin held the hem of the bride's dream dress in its mermaid style.

Pearl Walker carefully let go of the fabric and made explicit notes for the seamstress. There could be no miscommunications when it came to this dress. This dress had to be perfect, because it would belong to Pearl's sister Bethany.

The dress which hung in its bag just beyond her, on the rack, was for her cousin's future bride, Susan. That made two Walker brides having weddings in a span of two months. Who was next she wondered?

Her vote was on Lydia Morgan, her cousin Eric's other cousin, and a childhood friend of hers. Well, perhaps Pearl shouldn't consider they were friends back then. Lydia was studious and Pearl was a little bit of a wild child. Though, she thought, as she looked in the full-length mirror to her right, she certainly didn't look like one now.

Her suit was Vera Wang and it made her look the part of a successful business woman, owning her own bridal boutique. She kept her hair pinned up, that too made her look smart, she thought. Pearls had replaced the long ago black rubber bracelets that had lined her arm. A French manicure gave her nails a clean look, not like the black paint of years ago. A tattoo on her thigh wasn't seen, but there were traces of the bad girl that still lingering under the blonde façade of the business woman.

She heard the bell over the front door of her shop chime. Careful not to drop Bethany's dress, she stood and walked to the front.

Standing, all six-foot-four of him, very uncomfortable with his hands in the front pockets of his jeans, was Eric's half-brother Tyson Morgan.

"Hey, Ty. Did you come to get fitted for that tux finally?"

"Yeah. Don't know why they want me in their wedding. Don't they have professionals to do that?"

She smiled sweetly as she studied him. He was a country boy, that was for sure. Worn out work boots and faded jeans. His T-shirt might have seen better days and his hair peeked out around the edges of his baseball cap, which too got plenty of wear.

"They chose you to be in the wedding because you're important to them," she said.

"I spent most my life hating the Walker family, no offense."

"None taken."

"Who could have known I was related to one? Damn if that makes the least bit of sense ever, huh?"

"Come on back. Let's get you measured."

She walked toward her fitting area with the three-way mirror and platform. As she gathered her tape measure, she thought about that Walker-Morgan feud. It had been fueled for as long as she could remember. It was started over land rights early at the turn of last century and the battle continued until about ten months ago. It had become quite a shock to Tyson to find that the mother that abandoned him had been the same woman who married into the Walker family—Eric's mother. She'd been a troubled soul, but forty years later her *mistakes* had brought the two families together.

Now here stood the handsome Morgan man in her bridal shop. Truly this was something Pearl had never thought would happen either.

"What size are your shoes?"

A flash of annoyance crossed over Tyson's face. "Why?"

Pearl affixed her professional smile. "I carry a stock of dress shoes in back. If I take your measurements in the appropriate shoes, then I can assure that the tuxes will fit correctly."

"What's wrong with my boots?"

Keeping the smile in place, she replied, "Susan has requested that all the groomsmen wear dress shoes."

"Well, hell, no one mentioned that."

"Honestly, it won't take but a moment here. What size?"

She was sure he blurted out the number thirteen. She gave him a nod and disappeared into the back to find the appropriate sized shoe.

Men were usually more uncomfortable taking off their shoes in front of her than they were to take off their clothes. She could only assume that Tyson would be the same.

He was turned away from the mirror when she returned. She handed him the box containing the shoes.

"Here you go. Try these."

"I really think it would be fine if we…"

"Can I get you a soda or a bottle of water?" Men were also usually more comfortable with a bottle in their hands. Though she steered from keeping beer in the store, this was something she had studied.

"Uh, sure. Coke?"

"You put on the shoes. I'll get you one."

Again, she left him alone in the dressing area and ducked into the back room to retrieve the drink. Her refrigerator was full of sodas and water. She specifically purchased soda in bottles so that men could have that feel in their hands. If it were a woman she was trying to ease, she'd have poured the soda into a nice glass with ice.

When she figured she'd given him enough time, she walked back into the dressing area.

"Here you go," she handed out the bottle and smiled, acknowledging the shoes which were now on his feet.

"Thanks." He took the soda and twisted off the top. "Do you have men in here a lot?" he asked as he squirmed under her assessing look.

"Everyday. It's a normal event here. But like I said you'll be out in a few moments."

She draped the tape measure around the back of her neck and retrieved her measurement notebook and a pencil.

"I'm going to start with your shoulders."

He gave her a grunt of approval and she went to work.

Seriously, no one had ever asked him to do anything so uncomfortable in his entire life. And here he was, standing in a dress shop, in borrowed shoes, letting a Walker measure him.

In the mirror, he watched her move a step stool into place behind him and step up. She took the tape measure from around her neck, then ran it from one side of his shoulders to the other. The tingle of her fingers resonated through his shirt and down through his skin.

He bit down hard to control his body from flinching, gripping tightly to the bottle of soda in his hand.

"Now, I'll do your arm," her voice was soft and her breath was warm on his neck.

She held her hand at the top of his shoulder and just as she'd done across his back, she slid her hand delicately down his arm until she reached his wrist.

How quickly did she say this was going to take? Tyson was thinking he'd need a much stiffer drink than a soda when this was done.

Moving to the other arm, then his chest, it gave him the chance to catch the scent of her perfume.

Tyson clenched his toes in the borrowed shoes and closed his eyes as she reached her arms around his waist, her body brushing against his.

She took the measurement quickly and then wrote it down in the notebook she'd laid at her feet.

"Why couldn't I just tell you my pant size and my coat size? Really you have to measure everyone?" he asked, noticing she was kneeling before him and not rising.

Every person is built differently, even if they are the same *size*," she said using air quotes to emphasize her point.

Well, now how was he supposed to take that comment with her reaching her hands toward his crotch?

Realizing he was thinking just a bit too much about where her hands were going to travel, he stumbled back, nearly falling from the small platform she had him standing on.

"Sorry. I guess this is making me a little uncomfortable."

She smiled sweetly up at him. He didn't think it was possible to like a Walker, let alone find one extremely attractive, but damn if those blue eyes weren't burning right through him.

"Two more measurements," she promised.

Tyson clenched his fist at his side and closed his eyes as he felt her hand on the inside of his thigh.

"Okay, all done."

He realized he held his breath too.

"Good."

She stood and made her notes. "You can change your shoes back now."

He gave her a nod and went to the nearest chair to sit, setting the bottle of soda on the small table between the chairs. "You really do that every day? I mean, isn't that like feeling up men for a living?"

She chuckled. "If that's what you think I was doing."

Yeah, that was exactly what he was thinking *of* her doing while she was touching him.

He pulled off the shoes and tucked them into the box trying to control his thoughts.

"I kinda think I need a drink now." He'd said it louder than he'd meant to and he noticed her smiling and the heat in her cheeks. Maybe he should have kept it to himself.

"I'll let Susan know all the tuxes have been measured for," she said turning toward him.

"I was the last one, huh?"

"You were my hold out. I thought I was going to have to come out to your house. This might cause for some kind of celebration."

Now he could feel the heat rise in his own cheeks. Having his body measured at her store was bad enough. Had she done that in his own house…well, it was better to just stop thinking about it because now, looking at her in her perfect suit the image what they could have done was too vivid.

"Well, I guess we're done. I should go," he said after he pulled on his boots.

She looked up at him, those blue eyes burning right into him. The shimmering gloss on her lips only accentuated the fullness of them.

God, what was he thinking?

"Are you still going for that drink?" she asked and he had to think about what he'd said to prompt that.

"Oh, right. The drink. I think I'd better." Her eyes were still locked on him. "Would you like to join me?"

He watched as she licked her lips, then bit down on the bottom one with her perfectly white teeth. "I thought you'd never ask. Let me get my things."

His lungs began to burn and he realized again, he was holding his breath as he watched her walk away. What was he doing? Pearl Walker had a certain reputation he remembered. And if he remembered correctly the prim and proper version that just felt him up wasn't it.

This just might end up being the most interesting night of his life.

Meet the Author

Bestselling Author Bernadette Marie is known for building families readers want to be part of. Her series *The Keller Family* has graced bestseller charts since its release in 2011, along with her other series and single title books. The married mother of five sons promises *Happily Ever After always*…and says she can write it, because she lives it.

When not writing, Bernadette Marie is shuffling her sons to their many events—mostly hockey—and enjoying the beautiful views of the Colorado Rocky Mountains from her front step. She is also an accomplished martial artist with a second degree black belt in Tang Soo Do.

A chronic entrepreneur, Bernadette Marie opened her own publishing house in 2011, *5 Prince Publishing,* so that she could publish the books she liked to write and help make the dreams of other aspiring authors come true too. Bernadette Marie is also the CEO of *Illumination Author Events.*

www.ingramcontent.com/pod-product-compliance
Lightning Source LLC
Chambersburg PA
CBHW030414020726
47493CB00003B/1066